PUFFIN BOOK

Gervase Phinn is a teacher, freelance lecturer, author, poet, educational consultant, school inspector, visiting professor of education and, last but by no means least, father of four. Most of his time is spent in schools with teachers and children.

He is the author of *The Other Side of the Dale*, *Over Hill and Dale* and *Head Over Heels in the Dales*. His poetry collections, *It Takes One to Know One*, *The Day our Teacher Went Batty* and *Family Phantoms*, are also available in Puffin.

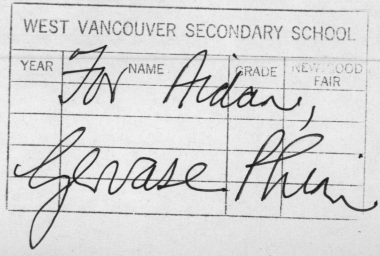

WEST VANCOUVER SECONDARY SCHOOL

YEAR	NAME	GRADE	NEW FOOD FAIR
For Aidan,			
Gervase Phinn			

Books by Gervase Phinn

DOMINIC'S DISCOVERY

For older readers
HEAD OVER HEELS IN THE DALES
THE OTHER SIDE OF THE DALE
OVER HILL AND DALE

Poetry
FAMILY PHANTOMS
IT TAKES ONE TO KNOW ONE
THE DAY OUR TEACHER WENT BATTY

GERVASE PHINN

Dominic's Discovery

PUFFIN

For Dominic

PUFFIN BOOKS

Published by the Penguin Group
Penguin Books Ltd, 80 Strand, London WC2R 0RL, England
Penguin Group (USA), Inc., 375 Hudson Street, New York, New York 10014, USA
Penguin Books Australia Ltd, 250 Camberwell Road, Camberwell, Victoria 3124, Australia
Penguin Books Canada Ltd, 10 Alcorn Avenue, Toronto, Ontario, Canada M4V 3B2
Penguin Books India (P) Ltd, 11 Community Centre, Panchsheel Park, New Delhi – 110 017, India
Penguin Books (NZ) Ltd, Cnr Rosedale and Airborne Roads, Albany, Auckland, New Zealand
Penguin Books (South Africa) (Pty) Ltd, 24 Sturdee Avenue, Rosebank 2196, South Africa

Penguin Books Ltd, Registered Offices: 80 Strand, London WC2R 0RL, England

www.penguin.com

First published 2004
4

The moral right of the author and illustrator has been asserted

Set in Monotype Baskerville with Perpetua Display
Typeset by Rowland Phototypesetting Ltd, Bury St Edmunds, Suffolk
Made and printed in England by Clays Ltd, St Ives plc

British Library Cataloguing in Publication Data
A CIP catalogue record for this book is available from the British Library

ISBN 0-141-31655-1

Contents

One

A Near Miss

'Dominic Dowson!' snapped Mr Merriman. 'You can be the most disorganized, disruptive and downright dangerous pupil I have ever had the misfortune to come across in my thirty years of teaching.'

Dominic, a small boy with a crown of close-cropped ginger hair, a face full of freckles and large wide eyes, peered up at the headteacher with a sad expression.

'And then at other times, you can be the most polite, pleasant, good-humoured and generous boy,' continued the headteacher, gripping the end of his desk so hard that his knuckles turned white. 'I just do not understand you. I cannot work you out. You are a complete enigma.' Mr Merriman shook his head dramatically. 'Do you know what an enigma is?'

Dominic stared up blankly. 'Is it an extinct South American bird with brightly-coloured feathers, sir?'

'No, it is not an extinct South American bird with brightly-coloured feathers,' groaned the headteacher, looking into the shiny innocent face before him.

Dominic noticed that the headteacher's face had turned a deep shade of red and his bald head was now pimpled with perspiration. His eyes seemed to be popping out like those on the picture of the chameleon on his classroom wall.

'An enigma is a conundrum, a puzzle, a perplexity, a riddle, something that cannot be understood, an unfathomable mystery.' Mr Merriman never used one word when several would do. He was one of those people Dominic's gran described as 'liking the sound of his own voice'. He was certainly getting into his stride now. 'And you are an enigma, Dominic, a human enigma,' continued the headteacher.

'Yes, sir,' said the boy quietly, still staring heaven-wards. He felt it best to say very little under the circumstances. He had been in the headteacher's room too many times to remember and knew that the best course of action was to stay silent and look as sad and sorry as possible. He wanted to tell Mr Merriman what had happened, how it really was not his fault, how he was only trying to be helpful, but he knew it would only make matters worse.

'One minute you are as good as gold and as nice as pie and the next minute you are up to your neck in hot water.' He also liked using expressions, did Mr Merriman. He was famous for them, in fact, and sometimes Dominic would count the number he could get in at assembly. The record was eighteen. 'Are you listening to what I'm saying, Dominic?'

'Yes, sir.'

'Because that's another of your problems. Head in the clouds, feet off the ground. Not listening to what people say.'

'Pardon, sir?'

'Do you see what I mean?' exclaimed Mr Merriman, slapping his hand flat on the desk top and making Dominic jump. 'You don't listen! It goes in one ear and out the other.'

'Yes, sir.'

'Every day this week you have been in my room to be hauled over the coals for getting into some mischief or being involved in some mishap – by Miss Pruitt, your form tutor; Mrs Simmonite, the cook; Mr Leech, the caretaker; Mrs Wellbeloved, the lollipop lady. The list goes on and on, doesn't it, like a never-ending saga of woe and worry, misery and misfortune?'

'Yes, sir.'

'On Monday it was the window and your incredible excuse: "I was just walking past it and it just sort of fell out".'

'Yes, sir.'

'How can a window-pane just fall out? There was

3

glass everywhere. Then, on Tuesday, the hamster escaped and you just happened to be the last one to have your hand in his cage. Mrs Simmonite is still suffering from shock at finding a rodent in the salad bowl, and Mrs Rashid has not been back to work since.'

'Yes, sir.'

'And I was given yet another of your grossly improbable explanations – that the hamster might have managed to flick up the catch by himself by watching how humans do it.'

'Yes, sir.'

'Then, on Wednesday, it was the fire extinguisher and an equally preposterous explanation that it could have been an earth tremor. You just happened to be walking past it, when it leapt off the wall. How you managed to knock it off in the first place is beyond me. The floor was covered in foam. It was like a skating rink down the corridor, children slipping and sliding. Mr Leech was at his wits' end, trying to clean up the mess.'

'Yes, sir.'

'And I do not need to remind you about Thursday and the incident at the pedestrian crossing – Jane Fairburn's clarinet and Mrs Wellbeloved's bent lollipop – do I?'

'No, sir.'

When Mr Merriman listed the catalogue of calamities, thought Dominic, it did sound as if he was a walking disaster, but there were perfectly good explanations. Well, *he* thought they were perfectly good explanations. The headteacher clearly did not.

Dominic's gran had once told him that he took after his Grandpa Dowson, who was accident prone. 'If there was a door, he'd bang into it; if there was a hole, he'd fall into it; if there was a banana skin, he'd slip on it. But there are worse things in the world,' she had said, 'than being a bit clumsy.' She also said that he had the same colourful imagination as his Grandpa Dowson.

'And you've always got some far-fetched, fanciful and fantastic reason for all these disasters, haven't you?' said Mr Merriman, and by the look on his face, he did not expect to be contradicted.

'Yes, sir.'

'Some extravagant tale, some weird and wonderful story, beyond the bounds of belief.'

'Yes, sir.'

'You're in another world most of the time, on another planet. The stories and excuses you invent. Your world seems to be full of aliens and monsters and ghosts and pirates and smugglers and highwaymen and I don't know what.'

'Yes, sir.'

'And you expect me to believe you? Do you think my brains are made of porridge, Dominic?'

'Yes, sir. I mean, no, sir.'

'You draw trouble towards you like a human magnet; you attract calamity like bees to a honey pot.'

'Yes, sir.'

5

'And now, today –' there was a great in-drawing of breath – 'shall we ever forget this fraught and fateful Friday? Did Miss Pruitt tell you to go into her storeroom?'

'No, sir.'

'Did she ask you to get the pots of powder paint from the top shelf?'

'No, sir.'

'Then, why in heaven's name did you? Clambering up like some inquisitive little monkey, balancing on a cardboard box, reaching out and bringing the whole lot toppling down like a ton of bricks.'

'I was just trying to be helpful, sir,' Dominic said. 'I didn't mean for the pots to fall, and if Miss Pruitt hadn't come in when she did, she wouldn't have got paint on her.'

'Got paint on her!' exclaimed Mr Merriman, waving his hand expansively as if trying to get rid of an irritating fly. 'Got paint on her! Dominic, she was covered from head to foot in paint. When I found her, she looked like your South American bird with brightly-coloured feathers. She was every colour of the rainbow.'

'Sorry, sir,' mumbled the boy, looking at his shoes.

Mr Merriman sighed dramatically. 'Dominic, Dominic. What am I going to do with you?'

'I don't know, sir.'

'And what am I going to do about the school trip next week?'

'I don't know, sir.'

'Miss Pruitt is not at all happy about taking you, you know that, Dominic?'

'Yes, sir.'

'She is extremely angry about what happened.'

'Yes, sir.'

'And she feels that, should she take you, you will be a danger to everyone and to yourself.'

'Yes, sir.'

'Dominic! Will you stop agreeing with me all the time. Just be quiet and listen.'

'Yes, sir.'

'The mind boggles at what you might get up to, a week away from school in a youth hostel on the Yorkshire coast. Anything could happen.' Mr Merriman paused for effect. 'And it's fruitless for me to ask you to promise to behave yourself, to turn over a new leaf, be on your best behaviour, because I have done that in the past, until I am blue in the face, and it's made not a blind bit of difference. You can promise to behave until the cows come home, as far as I'm concerned, but it cuts no ice with me.'

'Yes, sir.' Mr Merriman was certainly on form with his expressions that morning, thought Dominic. He must have broken the all-time record.

The headteacher sat down, placed his elbows on his desk, and stared up at the boy standing before him. 'So, I'm in two minds whether or not to let you go.'

'Yes, sir.'

'I think it might be better if you stayed at school and joined the class below for the week. Then I can

7

keep my eye on you and make sure you stay out of mischief.'

Dominic was quiet and looked at his shoes. He had not expected that bombshell. He imagined that it would be a good telling-off as usual, not being told he would have to miss the school trip. He had looked forward to the school visit to the coast for ages. When Miss Pruitt had first announced that the class was to spend a week in a youth hostel by the sea, Dominic's heart had jumped with excitement. Then he had thought of the cost. He knew that his mum probably couldn't afford it. When he mentioned the trip to his mum, sort of casually over tea, she had said she would think about it. But Gran had come to the rescue straight away and said of course he should go. She had dipped into her 'fund for emergencies'. Mum had made up the difference and the contents of his piggy bank would be enough for his pocket money. Dominic had drifted off to sleep every night since then thinking of the week at Thundercliff Bay. The very name – Thundercliff Bay – conjured up pirates and smugglers, buried treasure and galleons of gold. The trip would be fantastic.

'Lost for words for once in your life, are you?' said the headteacher now. 'Standing there as if butter wouldn't melt in your mouth. Has the cat got your tongue? What do *you* think I should do with you?'

Dominic looked at him with a melancholy face. He could feel his eyes filling with tears. He sniffed and rubbed his eyes. *It is true*, he thought to himself,

I always seem to be in some trouble or other. He didn't look for it – it found him.

'It might be for the best to keep me at school, sir,' replied Dominic in a trembling voice.

'Don't you want to go on the school trip to Thundercliff Bay?' asked the headteacher in a calmer voice.

'Yes, sir, I'd love to go. I've been looking forward to it for ages.'

'Then why don't you stay out of trouble?' sighed the headteacher, wiping his bald head with the flat of his hand. 'I know you're not a bad lad at heart, Dominic. You collected more than any pupil in your class on the sponsored walk to raise funds for the children's hospice, and I received several very complimentary letters about you from the senior citizens, after you'd taken the harvest baskets to the residential home. Of course, I found out later that you'd eaten half the produce on the way, but you certainly cheered up the old folk. They took quite a shine to you. You can be a very likeable lad when you want to be. The trouble is, you always seem to be in some sort of bother.'

Dominic sniffed and wiped away a tear.

Mr Merriman breathed out heavily and shook his head. 'All right, return to your class and I'll have a word with Miss Pruitt at afternoon break and I'll let you know at the end of the day what we have decided.' He watched the boy head for the door. He shook his head wearily and sighed. 'An enigma.'

Miss Pruitt was waiting for Dominic to return. She was a tall, lean woman with thick glasses, a pained expression and unnaturally bright golden hair – the result of the pot of yellow paint that had cascaded on to her that morning. Her face had a distinct blue tinge to it – the effect of the pot of turquoise paint that had exploded before her in the storeroom. Her hands were a pale, supernaturally green colour – the consequence of her trying to brush the yellow and the blue paint off her clothes. The class stopped writing and looked up when Dominic entered the room.

'Don't all stop what you're doing,' said Miss Pruitt sharply. 'Get on with your work. Dominic, you will find a worksheet on your table.'

The teacher watched the boy closely, as a hungry cat might watch a mouse. Dominic returned to his desk with a mournful countenance and sagging shoulders, and set about answering the questions. His best friend, Michael Chan, who was sitting opposite him, gave him a little smile. As Dominic bit his bottom lip to stop himself crying, he caught Miss Pruitt's eye and thought he saw a glimmer of sympathy.

Dominic liked Miss Pruitt. She was always cheerful and her lessons were really interesting. Once, when it had been her birthday, he had brought her a bunch of bright daffodils. He had told her that the daffodils had reminded him of that poem that she had once read to the class about 'wandering lonely as a cloud' and seeing 'hosts of golden daffodils'. She had been really pleased until she had found out that the flowers had been plucked from Mr Leech's garden. Dominic recalled the dreadful afternoon when the caretaker had stormed into the classroom, ballooning with anger. He had pointed at the stolen daffodils which adorned the teacher's desk, then had snatched them up furiously and stomped out. Talk about 'wandering lonely as a cloud': Mr Leech had thundered out of the room like a charging rhinoceros with toothache.

Dominic remembered another occasion when Christopher Wilkinson had started school and Miss Pruitt had picked him to help the new boy settle in. She had said he was just the one to make Christopher feel welcome. Of course, he had got into an argument with the new boy by the end of the day about which was the best football team – Sheffield Wednesday or Sheffield United – and the two of them had to be pulled apart by Mrs Wellbeloved. The crossing-patrol warden had arrived in the school, hot, flustered and angry, wielding her lollipop like a crazed Viking in one hand and the two dusty, wriggling combatants in the other.

Then there was the time he had brought a hedgehog into school and with it a whole host of jumping fleas. Everyone had been scratching all day.

The great thing about Miss Pruitt, thought Dominic, *is that when she tells you off, she never shouts or gets angry or waves her arms about like the headteacher, and once she has told you off, that is the end of the matter. She never brings it up again. She never keeps reminding you of it, like Mr Merriman.*

After a few minutes, Miss Pruitt approached

Dominic's desk and, leaning over him, asked in a whisper that was loud enough for most of the class to hear, what the headteacher had said to him.

'He said it would be better, miss, if I stayed at school next week and not go on the trip.'

Miss Pruitt looked surprised. 'Did he?'

'Yes, miss. He said, you said that I'm a danger to everyone and to myself.'

'Yes, I did say that,' began the teacher, 'but –'

'And that I draw trouble towards me like a magnet.'

'Well, you certainly do that, but –'

'And that I attract calamity like a honey pot attracts bees.'

'Mr Merriman's not far off the mark there, Dominic, but –'

'So, he thinks it would be better if I joined the class below next week while you are on the school trip to Thundercliff Bay.'

Nathan Thomas, on the next table, nudged his neighbour and whispered something which made his small companion snigger.

'Nathan Thomas!' snapped Miss Pruitt. 'Get on with your work and stop eavesdropping. And that goes for you as well, Darren Wilmott. It is impolite to listen to other people's private conversations and not nice to laugh at other people's misfortunes. Now Dominic,' she continued in a quieter voice, 'I did say that you could be a very trying and troublesome boy, but I didn't think Mr Merriman would ban you from coming on the school trip. I assumed that he

12

would just give you a good telling-off and leave it at that.'

'It's probably for the best, miss.'

'What's probably for the best?' asked the teacher.

'That I should stay at school next week, miss.'

'I shall decide whether it is or whether it is not for the best, Dominic,' replied Miss Pruitt, bristling. 'Don't you want to go to Thundercliff Bay with us?'

'Yes, miss, I'd love to. I've been looking forward to it for ages.'

'Well, I'll have a word with Mr Merriman at afternoon break, but I want you to promise me that you will be on your very, very best behaviour if we do decide to let you go.'

Nathan Thomas made a sort of grunting noise followed by a 'Huh'.

'Is there something wrong with your voice, Nathan?' asked Miss Pruitt, looking over the top of her glasses.

'No, miss,' replied the boy, smirking like the cat that got the cream.

'Then stop making that peculiar noise and get on with your work. You sound like an anteater with sinusitis. And take that silly grin off your face. One day the wind might change and your face will stay like that.' The teacher turned her attention back to Dominic. 'Now, I am still very angry with you, Dominic, about what happened in the storeroom.'

'Yes, miss.'

'And if I can persuade Mr Merriman to let you go

to Thundercliff Bay, then you must promise me you will be on your very best behaviour.'

'I will, miss.' Dominic gave a great wide grin and stared up at the teacher's blue face. Michael Chan smiled and gave a thumbs-up sign.

'Miss?' said Dominic.

'Yes?'

'I'm sorry about the paint.'

When Miss Pruitt had returned to her desk, Dominic's other friend, Sean Murphy, pushed a note across the table to him which read: 'I'm really glad you'll be going. It wouldn't be the same without you.'

Dominic nodded and smiled back at him. 'Thanks Smurph,' he mouthed.

Later that morning, when Miss Pruitt was busy trying to rid herself of the remains of the powder paint, Nathan Thomas leaned over his desk.

'Well, I hope "Mighty Mouth" Merriman doesn't let you go,' he said nastily. 'You might wrap "Dizzy Lizzy" Miss Pruitt round your little finger with your, "It's probably for the best that I don't go on the trip, miss," and your "I'm sorry about the paint, miss." But you won't get around old Merriman that easily.'

At afternoon break Dominic was summoned to the headteacher's room. Mr Merriman sat at his desk looking stern, his fingers steepled before him.

'You wanted to see me, sir?' said Dominic nervously.

'I don't know what you said to Miss Pruitt, Dominic,' said the headteacher, 'but she's been to see me, pleading your cause and asking me to let you go on the school trip next week.'

'Great!' gasped Dominic.

'Now, don't think the incident with the paint has been forgotten because when you return there will be various jobs about the school for you to do to make amends. And don't think you will be having an easy time next week. As you are aware, your class is joining up with a class from Cransworth Junior School in the charge of Mr Risley-Newsome, whose reputation goes before him. From what I have heard of Mr Risley-Newsome, he stands no nonsense, no nonsense at all. I have mentioned your name to him, just now on the telephone, so he will be keeping a special eye on you and making quite certain that you remain out of trouble. Is that clear?'

'Yes, sir.' Dominic's smile stretched from ear to ear. 'Thanks, sir.'

Mr Merriman had not had a particularly pleasant conversation on the telephone with the teacher in question, if truth be known.

'I may be old-fashioned,' Mr Risley-Newsome had told Mr Merriman pompously, 'but I believe in high standards of behaviour. It is essential that accidents do not occur and that children follow instructions to the letter. I do pride myself on my excellent safety record.'

'Really,' Mr Merriman had replied wearily.

'And I mean to maintain that excellent safety record,' Mr Risley-Newsome had announced. 'So

15

have no fear, I shall be watching the Dowson boy with eagle eyes.'

Later in the staff room, Mr Merriman had shared his reservations about Mr Risley-Newsome with a gloomy-looking Miss Pruitt. 'He does sound a bit of a stick in the mud, Elizabeth,' he had remarked. 'A trifle on the serious side, a rather intense man by the sound of him, but I am sure you will get on famously.' There was no conviction in his voice.

Miss Pruitt had smiled weakly. 'I hope so,' she had said. 'I do hope so.'

Two

Gran's Gold Sovereign

'Now, are you sure you've got everything?' Dominic's mum was poking her head round his bedroom door the Sunday night before the school trip to Thundercliff Bay.

'Yep.'

'Socks?'

'Yep.'

'Shirts?'

'Yep.'

'Jumpers?'

'Yep.'

'Waterproofs?'

'Yep.'

'Boots?'

'Stop worrying, Mum,' replied Dominic. 'I've got everything. I've checked, double-checked and triple-checked.'

'Yes, well I've heard that one before. You'd forget your head if it wasn't screwed on. I know you of old. I remember when we went to Blackpool and you forgot your swimming trunks and then you left your camera on the bus coming home.'

'Honest, Mum, I've got everything.'

'Well, just so long as you're sure. Anyway, tea's ready, so fasten up your case and come on down.'

Dominic crammed the last article of clothing into the small, brown, rather battered case.

'That case has seen better days,' his mum said. 'I remember your gran had it when I was a girl. It was old then.'

'It's probably an antique,' said Dominic, snapping the catches shut. 'But it's fine, Mum.'

'Oh, it's an antique all right,' chuckled his mum. 'And that rucksack you borrowed from your Uncle Michael looks as if it's been through two world wars.'

'I told you, Mum, it's not worth buying a new case and rucksack just for one trip. I'll probably never use them again.'

Dominic's mum wished she could have afforded to buy new ones but money was a bit short at the moment and it was coming up to Christmas. She smiled at

Dominic. He was a good lad. He wasn't hard to please. 'Come on, then, tea's ready.'

'I'll just make double sure I've got everything,' he said.

Dominic lived with his mum and his gran in a small red-bricked terraced house with a greasy grey roof and small square windows. The kitchen looked out on a cracked, grey concrete yard with an outdoor store, and the front door opened directly on to the pavement and the busy, dusty main road. There wasn't very much room in the house. His mum had one bedroom, his gran another and he had the small boxroom with just enough space for a bed, bedside table and a wardrobe. He often wished he lived in a great big rambling house like Nathan Thomas's, with its curved, sweeping, gravel drive, huge pointed roof, large lawned garden and a bedroom overlooking the golf course. It was his next-best-favourite dream.

His very favourite dream was about his dad. He dreamed that one day, his dad – whom he couldn't even remember – would walk through the door. He'd be really famous and rich and drive a huge car and live in a mansion with a swimming pool, and a bathroom with solid gold taps.

Dominic's mum never talked about his dad. She had told him that he had left when Dominic was little and that was that. When he mentioned his dad, his mum quickly changed the subject. Gran had told him once, when he had gone on and on about him, that his father was a very quiet, serious man – a dreamer, not cut out for family life, someone who just couldn't settle down, who had to be on the move all the time.

Dominic often thought to himself that he must be a bit like his dad. He loved to dream as well, and would go to sleep at night thinking of all sorts of exciting adventures. He knew deep down that his dreams would remain dreams, that they were as fantastic and far-fetched as the ones Mr Merriman was always going on about – extravagant tales, weird and wonderful stories which would never come true, but it never stopped him dreaming.

Dominic's mother worked hard and did her best for him, but she always seemed to be short of money. He knew she had found it hard to pay for the trip to Thundercliff Bay. Perhaps it would have been better if he had, after all, stayed at school for the week. At least it would have saved her the money. He snapped out of his reverie when he heard his mum's voice at the bottom of the stairs.

'Dominic! Will you get down here now! Your tea's on the table.'

In the living room, Dominic's gran was sitting in her chair, with a tray on her knee, watching television.

'Hello, love,' she said as Dominic entered the room. Her eyes always brightened up when she saw him. She called him 'the apple of her eye' and sprang to his defence whenever he got into trouble. Like the episode with the rock bun, the seagull, the mad woman and the chihuahua. But that was another story.

'Hi, Gran,' Dominic said cheerfully.

'Someone's in a good mood.'

'I am,' replied her grandson, giving her a kiss.

'Are you all set, then?'

'Yep, all packed up and ready to go,' he said, heading for the small kitchen.

'And you've got everything?' she asked.

'Yep,' he replied, emerging a moment later with a plateful of steaming chips and sausages.

'Have you got plenty of clean underpants?'

'Yes, Gran, loads and loads, enough to sink a battleship.'

'That'll do,' came his mum's good-natured voice from the kitchen.

'Because if you get knocked down, you don't want to arrive at hospital with dirty underwear on, do you?' said Gran.

Dominic's mum appeared. 'Don't give him ideas, Mother,' she warned. 'He's not going to get knocked down. There are going to be no accidents.' She looked knowingly at her son. 'Are there, Dominic?'

'You never can tell, what with all these busy roads, Maureen,' continued Gran undeterred. 'You can't have too many pairs of underpants, that's what I always say. I remember when I was at school, Jimmy Sargeson was sewn into his vest for the winter. My goodness, you knew if you had to sit next to him. Pooh, he did smell, and no mistake. What the doctors would have thought if he had had an accident and been taken to hospital. Then there was Ethel Clegg, wet her knickers on her way to school and Miss Price, our teacher, made her put them on the old stove in the classroom to dry out. Ooooh, the steam and the smell. I remember it to this day. And poor Ethel, sniffling and snuffling, she was so embarrassed. We might not have had much money when I was a girl but we always had clean underwear.'

'Gran, I'm trying to have my tea, here,' said Dominic laughing, 'and all you can talk about is dirty underwear.'

'It's always best to be on the safe side and pack a few extra undergarments,' persisted Gran. 'That's what I always say. You can never be too sure. Anyway, Dominic, fetch me my bag, will you?'

'If you've got a clean pair of underpants in there,' Dominic told her mischievously, 'I don't need them.'

'Go on with you,' chuckled Gran. 'Go and get my bag.'

'He's just started his tea, Mother,' sighed her daughter. 'Can't he get your bag later?'

'It'll only take a minute, Maureen. I'll forget if I don't do it now.'

Dominic put down his plate and scrambled up the stairs, returning a moment later with a large, black, battered handbag which he placed next to his gran. She gave him the tray from her lap and began rootling in the bag until she found a shiny pound coin which she held up.

'Whatever's that?' she teased.

'A pound, Gran.'

'And I wonder who's it for?'

'Me, Gran,' said Dominic.

'Is it?'

'Yes, Gran.'

'This is for the best boy in the whole wide world. I wonder who that can be?'

'Me, Gran,' replied Dominic, playing along with her and laughing.

'Is it? Well, you better have it, then,' she said. 'To buy an ice cream.'

'Thanks, Gran,' he said.

'And are you too big to give your gran a kiss?' she asked.

Dominic wrapped his arms round his gran and gave her a great kiss. She smelt of flowers and sandalwood soap, and her cheeks, soft and wrinkled as an old apple, had a light-brown powder on them as if she had sprinkled a dusting of cinnamon on them. Dominic immediately thought of Miss Pruitt. He saw that there were tears in his gran's eyes. She once told him that people sometimes cried when they were happy.

'You know, Dominic, when I was a girl my grandma had a pound coin. She used to clean for an old gentleman called Mr Lloyd. A doctor he was. Used to have a silver-topped cane. When he died it was left to her in his will.'

'The silver-topped cane?' asked Dominic.

'No, no, the pound coin.'

'He only left her a pound!' exclaimed Dominic. 'One single measly pound!'

'It doesn't sound a lot now, does it,' said Gran, 'but it was worth quite a lot of money in those days. A pound went a long way when I was a girl. I used to love looking at that coin, all bright and golden. It was called a sovereign. Shiny, it was, with the head of the old queen on one side and St George fighting the dragon on the other. It was worth its weight in gold, not like these modern coins. My gran kept it in her purse and brought it out sometimes to show me. I'd hold it in my hand and curl my little fingers over it and she'd say that one day it would be mine.'

'Have you still got it, Gran?' asked Dominic.

'No, love, I haven't. I never did get it.'

'What happened?' asked Dominic.

His gran sighed and gave a small, sad smile. 'Well, love, we were short of money. We had to eat and we had to have shoes. Nothing's changed, has it? My grandma had to spend it.'

'Well, when I become rich and famous, I'll get you a sovereign,' said Dominic. 'Real gold, and you can wear it round your neck on a great, big, thick, golden chain.'

'You're a good boy, Dominic,' said his gran. 'I'll miss you next week. It'll be very quiet around here without you.'

'I'm only going for five days, Gran,' he told her.

'Well, don't go getting into any bother, will you.'

'No, Gran.'

'And stay away from seagulls.'

'Yes, Gran.'

'Mother, will you let him get his tea. It's going cold,' said Dominic's mum.

'It will be like a cemetery around here without my Dominic,' said Gran thoughtfully.

'A bit of peace and quiet, for a change,' said his mum, smiling. She, too, would miss him.

'You'll make your mum and me very proud one day,' said his gran. 'Now, are you sure you've got plenty of clean underpants?'

It was a cold, clear Monday morning when Dominic opened his eyes. Through the small window, pale winter sunlight lit up the bedroom like theatre spotlights. Early morning traffic could be heard rumbling and grumbling along the road outside. He glanced at the small plastic clock in the shape of a dinosaur (a present from Gran) on the bedside cabinet, yawned massively, snuggled down under the blankets and buried his head in the pillow. Seven o'clock – time enough before he braved the chilly room.

This week at Thundercliff Bay is going to be terrific, Dominic thought to himself. The children, seventeen from Cransworth Juniors together with his class from St Jude's, were setting off that morning, returning the following Friday, so that was five full days off school. No long assemblies, no lining up in the playground in the cold, no maths and no school dinners for a full week.

He wondered what the pupils from Cransworth would be like. Cransworth was at the other side of the town, where there were all the big houses and the park and the playing field. Gran used to say that that was where all the rich people lived. *The Cransworth pupils will probably be really snooty and big-headed*, thought Dominic, *with loads of spending money and expensive equipment. Then there is their teacher – Mr Risley-Newsome.* Mr Merriman's words echoed in his head: 'he stands no nonsense, no nonsense at all.'

Dominic banished such thoughts from his mind. Nothing was going to spoil his week away at the seaside. He examined the cracks on the ceiling and imagined the long walks along the sandy beaches, clifftop rambles, a visit to Robin Hoods Bay, hikes across the lonely moors, maybe a trip on a boat and then there would be the evenings – telling ghost stories, midnight feasts, exchanging jokes. Miss Pruitt had let them choose the friends they wanted to share a room with and Dominic had picked his two best pals – Sean Murphy (Smurph) and Michael Chan. He was glad he was not in the same room as Nathan Thomas. That would have been really, really awful.

'Dominic! Dominic! Are you up yet?' It was Mum's usual early morning call. 'It's gone seven o'clock, you know! Your breakfast's on the table. Come on, hurry up, slowcoach, or you'll be late.'

'I'm just getting up!' he shouted, sliding further beneath the warm covers and still staring at the cracks on the ceiling. They looked like hundreds of criss-crossing paths on a lunar surface. He wondered if the food would really be as good as Miss Pruitt had described. Miss Brewster, the warden of the youth hostel where they would be staying, their teacher had told them, was famous for her fabulous food. And then there was the village shop, handy for sweets and crisps, and Robin Hoods Bay with all that candyfloss, sticky pink seaside rock, ice cream and slabs of thick, chewy toffee. Dominic pulled the blankets round him and smiled at the thought of the week in Thunder-cliff Bay.

'Dominic! I shan't tell you again, young man. Will you get up! You'll be late.' His mother's voice was louder and sharper now.

He yawned widely, sat up, stretched expansively and clambered from his bed, shivering. *Yes*, he thought to himself, *this week is going to be great!* Then, he caught sight of the bedside clock.

'Crikey!' he cried. 'I *shall* be late!' He rushed for the bathroom with the most dreadful thoughts spinning through his head. He would arrive at school to see the coach pulling off in a cloud of exhaust fumes and Nathan Thomas and Darren Wilmott smiling smugly and waving slowly from the back window. Mr Merriman would be there at the gate to greet him, stern-faced like an undertaker and with another of his famous expressions: 'You'll be late for your funeral, you will!'

It took Dominic fifteen minutes to go to the toilet, have a shower, wash and comb his hair, clean his teeth and get dressed. He was so relieved that he had packed his case the previous evening.

Downstairs, breakfast was on the table.

'What time is Michael's dad collecting you?' asked his mum.

'Eight o'clock,' replied Dominic, spraying half-eaten cornflakes everywhere.

'It's nearly that now. You'll have to get your skates on, young man. And how many times do I have to tell you not to talk with your mouth full?' his mother told him.

'Well, how am I supposed to answer your question,' he spluttered, 'with my mouth closed? Pretty impossible, I should say, Mother dear, unless of course I happen to be a world-famous ventriloquist or I have some special psychic powers which —'

'That'll do, clever clogs,' said his mum. 'You've always got an answer for everything, haven't you? Now, be quick, Michael's father will be here in a minute.'

As soon as she had uttered the words, there was a *toot, toot, toot* outside the front door. 'You see,' said his mother, shaking her head. 'That's him now.'

'Crikey!' exclaimed Dominic for the second time that morning. 'He's dead on time and I haven't said goodbye to Gran yet. Tell Mr Chan I will be out in a second, will you, Mum?' Before she could answer, he was out of the door and scrabbling up the stairs.

Gran's room was shadowy and smelt of lavender polish and mothballs. Through the thick, flowery curtains, splinters of winter sunshine pierced the darkness. Dominic could make out the square, iron-framed

28

bed, deep cushiony armchair and Gran's old sideboard covered in photographs, china dishes, delicate, pale, porcelain figures of ladies with parasols, and little glass containers.

'Are you awake, Gran?'

'It'd take a corpse to sleep through all the racket this morning,' she said with good humour, sitting up and clicking on the bedside light. 'Now, have you got everything?'

'Everything,' replied Dominic. 'Including a year's supply of clean underpants.'

'Well, behave yourself and have a nice time and be careful near the sea and all those cliffs.'

'I will.'

'And stay well away from seagulls,' she chuckled. 'You remember last time we were at the seaside?'

'Will I ever forget,' said Dominic.

'And look after my case.'

'I will.'

'And be sure to send me a postcard.'

Dominic gave his gran a big kiss and rushed from the room. 'Bye, Gran!' he shouted as he disappeared.

Mr Chan was talking to Dominic's mum on the pavement when Dominic scuttled out of the door, case in hand, coat over his arm and rucksack strapped on his back. Michael was in the back of the car, beaming widely and bouncing up and down, looking as excited as Dominic felt. Mr Chan packed the small, battered, brown case and old khaki rucksack in the boot.

'Got everything, Dom?' he asked.

'Sure have, Mr Chan,' replied Dominic. He reached out and gave his mum a hug. 'Bye, Mum.'

'Bye, love,' she said.

'Let's get you both to the school,' said Michael's dad. 'Bye, Maureen.'

Dominic clambered into the back of the car, waved to his mum and to his gran, who was looking out from behind the curtain at her window, and soon they were speeding though the town traffic towards St Jude's.

Dominic was blissfully unaware that his walking boots were still behind the back door, where he had left them the night before.

Three
Grisly Beginnings

Children, surrounded by cases and rucksacks, were waiting in small knots in the playground when Dominic and Michael arrived at St Jude's Primary School. On seeing their friend, Sean Murphy, standing outside the school entrance, the two boys rushed to meet him.

'I was getting worried,' Sean said. 'I thought you might have overslept. Have you got everything?'

'You sound just like my mum,' replied Dominic, 'and if anyone else asks me if I have got everything, I shall explode.'

'Well, I realized I'd forgotten something on the way

here,' Sean told them. 'I remembered as soon as we were at the end of our street that I didn't put in a torch, and my dad wouldn't go back.'

'I've brought two,' said Dominic, sounding very pleased with himself. 'You can borrow one of mine, Smurph. My gran got me a new one, really powerful, and I've got a pocket torch as well. You can borrow that.'

'Thanks, Dom.'

'This is going to be great,' said Michael. 'I can't wait until we get to the seaside.'

'Me too,' said Dominic. 'Where's Miss Pruitt?' he asked suddenly, looking around him.

'She's in school with that teacher from Cransworth Juniors,' explained Sean, screwing up his face as if sucking a lemon, 'and he looks really, really horrible; I mean seriously grim and ghastly, like someone who's just been dug up after years and years underground. He's lanky and creepy – horror-film material!'

'My cousin's at Cransworth Juniors,' Michael told them. 'She says that Mr Risley-Newsome is really, really strict and nobody likes him.'

'He's probably OK,' said Dominic, more to reassure himself than his two friends. 'As Mr Merriman would no doubt say, "You should never judge a book by its cover. Looks aren't everything." Underneath "Old Grisly-Gruesome" is –' He stopped mid-sentence, for the person in question had made an appearance.

Mr Risley-Newsome emerged from the school fol-lowed by a weary-looking Miss Pruitt. She was dressed in a bright-pink padded anorak, electric-blue slacks, red gloves and matching scarf and orange boots, in stark contrast to the lanky figure beside her.

Her companion was a tall stick of a man with grizzled grey hair, a nibbled moustache, skin the colour of dripping and small penetrating eyes like chips of shiny green glass. He wore the sort of outfit one would expect an Antarctic explorer or a seasoned mountain climber to wear: a thick, dark-green, hooded anorak, fur-trimmed, and with numerous pockets and pouches; matching green-corduroy breeches; long grey socks and heavy, thick, rubber-soled boots, neatly laced up and newly polished. Round his neck dangled a square of plastic to hold his maps, a compass on a cord and a silver whistle. He was prodding a clipboard with a gloved finger and nodding vigorously to Miss Pruitt, who looked tired out and harassed already.

Dominic took a deep breath. 'I do not like the look of him,' he whispered, slowly and deliberately. 'I do not like the look of him at all.'

'I told you,' said Sean in a self-satisfied tone of voice, his hand cupped round his mouth as if the person in question might hear him.

'I don't like the look of him either,' agreed Michael. 'He's like the son of Dracula. I'm not turning my back on him: he might bite my neck.'

'I know,' said Sean Murphy. 'Ghastly and grisly, isn't he?'

'He's like something out of *The Curse of the Mummy's Tomb*,' said Dominic under his breath. 'Nobody has skin that colour and those glittery eyes, they give me the creeps!'

Mr Risley-Newsome peered over in the children's direction and glowered.

'Do you think he heard us?' asked Sean.

Dominic smiled back at the teacher and waved. The teacher scowled and turned to face Miss Pruitt. 'The coach should be here by now,' he said in a low growl of a voice. 'I do wish people would be prompt.'

'It's not quite eight thirty, by my watch,' replied Miss Pruitt.

'It is by mine,' Mr Risley-Newsome told her, consulting the huge timepiece on his wrist. 'And my watch is never wrong.'

Miss Pruitt looked heavenwards but refrained from responding. She could see that the trip to Thundercliff Bay would be something of an ordeal.

When the coach pulled up outside the school gates, Mr Risley-Newsome gave three sharps blasts on his silver whistle and walked into the centre of the school yard. All the pupils from Cransworth Junior School made their way towards him like automata and formed a neat half-circle round him. The children from St Jude's and the bus driver, a round, jolly-faced individual, ambled in the teachers' direction.

'Look lively!' snapped Mr Risley-Newsome. 'We haven't got all day!' When all the children were assembled, he cleared his throat noisily and addressed them. 'My name is Mr Risley-Newsome. The children from Cransworth Junior School obviously know me and the children from St Jude's soon will. For the benefit of the children in my class, this is Miss Pruitt.' He gestured in the direction of the multicoloured apparition next to him. 'And this is our coach driver, Mr Barnett.'

'Hi kids!' cried the coach driver, holding up a large, fat hand as if stopping traffic. 'Just call me Stan. I don't want any of this "mister" malarkey.'

'Now, before we embark on our journey to Thundercliff Bay,' continued Mr Risley-Newsome, 'there are one or two ground rules about your behaviour on the coach, of which you all need to be aware. I have led school parties on coaches and trains, boats and planes, up mountains, down valleys, across moors and down dales, and therefore I know the procedures like the hairs on the back of my hand.' The children stared at his hairy hands intently. The word 'werewolf' came into Dominic's head.

'Follow my instructions and we will all have a pleasant, peaceful and trouble-free journey. Do not follow my instructions and I will come down on you like a ton of bricks. I hope I make myself perfectly clear.' Everyone, including Miss Pruitt and the bus driver, stared mutely.

'These are my do's and don'ts. One: keep the coach clean at all times. Crisp packets, sweet wrappers, cans and bottles and all other forms of rubbish will be deposited in this plastic bin liner and not on the floor or stuffed behind the seats.' Like a magician producing a rabbit from a hat, he plucked a large plastic bag from the rucksack strapped to his back.

'Two: if you feel sick – use the bucket.' He indicated a large, pale-green, plastic bucket which a large girl with ginger hair was holding like a handbag.

'Three: on the coach there will be no shouting, jumping up and down, moving about, singing, loud conversations or music of any kind.

'Four: there will be one stop on the way and no other unscheduled interruptions to the journey. Therefore, make sure you all have been to the toilet before you get on the coach. Are there any questions?'

When Dominic spoke up, Miss Pruitt looked as if she had been given a piece of dreadful news. Her mouth dropped open in shock, her shoulders sagged and her face took on a tragic expression.

'Can we get on the coach now, sir?' Dominic asked innocently.

'Excuse me?' snapped the teacher, bristling.

'I said can we get on the coach now, sir?' Dominic repeated.

'You *can* get on the coach,' replied Mr Risley-Newsome, smiling widely like a vampire about to sink its teeth into a victim. It was not a pleasant smile. 'You have the ability to get on the coach, the legs to carry you up the steps of the coach, but whether you *may* get on the coach is another matter altogether.'

'Pardon, sir?'

'You clearly are unaware, young man, of the difference between the verbs "can" and "may". Let me enlighten you. The word "can" is an auxiliary verb expressing an ability or knowledge of how to do something. The word "may" is another auxiliary verb expressing the possibility or the permission to do something. Is that clear?'

About as clear as mud, thought Dominic. 'Oh, yes, sir,' he replied sweetly.

'So you *can* indeed get on the bus but whether you *may* is another matter altogether.'

'So, can we get on the bus, then, sir?' asked Dominic.

'Did you hear a word of what I have I just said, you silly boy –' began Mr Risley-Newsome.

Miss Pruitt, who was finding this prolonged discussion quite tedious and tiresome, and wanting to get on her way, interrupted. 'We will all get on the coach in a minute, Dominic,' she said. 'Just have a little patience.'

Mr Risley-Newsome jumped as if someone had pricked him with a pin. 'Dominic!' he exclaimed and his face twisted into a leer. 'Dominic Dowson?'

'Yes, sir,' replied the boy, smiling widely 'That's me.'

'So you are Dominic Dowson, are you?' said Mr Risley-Newsome. 'Making your presence felt before we have even got on the coach? I have been warned about you, Dominic Dowson. I have it on good authority that you are a nuisance of the first order, a number one mischief maker, a storyteller, a "ne'er-do-well".'

He always does it, thought Michael, shaking his head.

He always manages to get into some sort of bother, does Dominic.
Why does it always have to be him, of all people, who is the first
one to open his mouth? Now 'Old Grisly-Gruesome' was
in a bad mood. Why couldn't his friend, just for once,
be quiet and not draw attention to himself? *But that*
wouldn't be Dominic, would it, he thought, *and I suppose*
that's why I like him.

Mr Risley-Newsome was still rambling on. 'Well, let
me tell you this, Dominic Dowson: I have my eye on
you.' He stooped and stared into the boy's eyes with
those sharp green, glittery chips of glass gleaming in
the sunlight. 'I shall be watching you like a hungry
hawk. Is that clear?'

'Yes, sir,' replied Dominic cheerfully. 'So, can we
get on the bus now, sir?'

'You *may* get on the bus when I say you *may*,' thundered Mr Risley-Newsome, 'and not before. And
when you do eventually get on the bus –'

'Which I hope won't be much longer,' said the
driver in an exasperated voice, 'because I was hoping
to miss the rush-hour traffic and arrive at Thundercliff
Bay before the sun sets.'

'As I was saying,' continued the teacher, ignoring the interruption, 'when you do eventually get
on the bus, you will sit at the front where I can see
you.'

Dominic's heart sank, but he was not going to give
Mr Risley-Newsome the satisfaction of seeing how
disappointed he was. He'd gone and put his foot in it
again, hadn't he? He'd opened his big mouth. He had

really wanted to sit on the back seat with Michael and Sean.

'Thank you, sir,' he replied, pretending to be pleased. 'There's more to see at the front and much more leg room.'

Mr Risley-Newsome gave him a crushing glare. 'And you will be in charge of the litter bag and the sick bucket. Now,' he continued, addressing the assembled pupils, 'stack your cases and rucksacks tidily on the pavement near the coach and line up in an orderly fashion.'

The children, whispering and sniggering, dispersed quickly.

'And quietly!' boomed Mr Risley-Newsome after them.

'Well,' observed the coach driver gloomily as he walked across the playground with Dominic and his friends, 'you're in for a fun-packed few days with that teacher of yours, and that's for sure!'

'He's not my teacher,' explained Dominic. 'Miss Pruitt's my teacher and I shall never complain about her again.'

'He's our teacher,' said a glum-looking boy with thick glasses, red hair and a sprinkling of freckles on his pale face, 'and he's a nightmare.'

'He never smiles, he never laughs, he never speaks quietly and he's always right,' said another Cransworth pupil, a tall black girl, with coloured braids in her hair. 'He shouts and spits and orders you about. Everybody's frightened of him – even the parents.'

'This trip's going to be a right barrel of laughs,' moaned Michael Chan.

'Best advice I can give,' said the red-haired boy, 'is say nothing, ask nothing and keep out of his way. Isn't that right, Velma?'

The girl nodded and sighed.

As they passed Nathan Thomas and Darren Wilmott, Dominic heard their sniggers.

'In charge of the rubbish bag and the sick bucket,' came a mocking, chortling voice from behind them. 'He couldn't have picked a better person. Dustbin Dowson, refuse collector and garbage man.'

'Yeah, Dustbin Dowson,' came Darren's familiar echo.

'Only jealous,' said Dominic, throwing back his head and assuming a swagger, 'because I've been made a monitor and am sitting at the front.'

Nathan Thomas persisted. 'Where did you get your gear from, Dowson? A charity shop?'

For the second time that morning Dominic did not wish to give his tormentor the satisfaction of seeing him upset by the remarks. His gran had always told him that when people make fun of you, take the wind out of their sails by not rising to the comments but to smile and shrug it off. It never fails to work. If you show them you are upset, then they persist. So, Dominic glanced behind him and looked at the two boys as he might at a tramp sitting on the street corner – a face full of distant pity. 'You are a very sad person, Nathan,' he said pleasantly. 'A very sad person.'

He noticed that Nathan's case was the slim, light-weight variety with brightly-coloured straps and little wheels and his rucksack looked brand new and expensive.

'It's like an old woman's case that –' started Nathan.

Before Dominic could reply, the bus driver stepped in. 'Just you keep your clever comments to yourself, sunshine,' he told Nathan, 'or you'll have me to deal with.' He turned back to Dominic. 'You can help me load up the cases, if you like, son.'

'I've got a case like yours,' Velma told Dominic, smiling.

As Mr Risley-Newsome checked everybody on to the coach, dramatically ticking the register on his clipboard, Dominic, Sean and Michael passed the cases and rucksacks to the driver to stow away in the luggage compartment of the coach. When the driver came to Nathan Thomas's elegant case, he threw it nonchalantly, but with such force, that it slid and skidded across the floor of the luggage compartment before crashing to a halt. The spanking new rucksack was propelled at even greater speed and bounced and rolled to the back before thudding against the side of the coach. The driver picked up Dominic's small, battered, brown case and placed it delicately in the luggage compartment as if it contained some priceless and delicate bone china, and then he smiled and winked at Dominic without a word.

When everyone was aboard, Mr Risley-Newsome

paced round the coach, peering underneath the chassis and kicking the tyres.

'Any problems?' asked the driver, who watched him with folded arms and an expression of distaste.

'I'm just checking to see if this vehicle is fully road-worthy,' replied the teacher blithely.

'Would you like to look under the bonnet?' asked the driver sarcastically. 'Or slide underneath to make certain the back axle is still there?'

'That won't be necessary,' Mr Risley-Newsome told him with a vague sweeping gesture of the hand. 'You will appreciate, Mr Barnett, that safety has to be a priority when it comes to taking children on school trips.'

'I do know that!' exclaimed the driver, his face turning red with irritation. 'I have taken umpteen school trips over the years without any problems and I've not had any complaints before.'

'I am not complaining, Mr Barnett, I am checking.'

'Well, you don't need to check. I gave the coach a thorough going-over yesterday as I always do before a school journey.'

'Excellent,' replied the teacher, clambering up the steps to the coach. 'Then you can go.'

Dominic, sitting on the front seat, heard Miss Pruitt mutter under her breath, 'You *may* go.'

Four

A Gruesome Journey

The coach pulled out of the lay-by at the front of the school, meandered through the busy morning traffic and was soon speeding along the motorway.

Mr Risley-Newsome sat with Miss Pruitt, directly behind the driver, on the front seat. Across the aisle, Dominic sat with the red-headed boy with the large glasses and freckles, cradling the sick bucket on his lap. He discovered that his companion's name was Gerald.

'Everybody calls me Ginger,' he told Dominic, rather sadly, 'but I like to be called Gerald.' He thought for a moment. 'But nobody does, though. They all call me Ginger.'

'I'll call you Gerald,' said Dominic.

'Thanks,' he said. 'I have to sit at the front because I get travel sick.'

'Well, you're sitting next to the right person, then. I'm in charge of the sick bucket. So any time you feel a bit queasy . . .'

'Thanks,' Gerald said, sighing. 'My mum says I'm a bit of a loner,' he continued. 'She says I ought to get out more, play football, go for rides on my bike, but I like reading and I make model aeroplanes. I've loads and loads of books and models. I like lying on my bed reading best.'

'I like reading,' said Dominic, slightly taken aback by the other boy's outburst. 'Adventure stories.'

'They're my favourite too.' Gerald looked a whole lot more cheerful now. 'My mum says I'm in a world of my own.'

'That's what my mum says about me,' Dominic told him. 'A bit of a dreamer.'

The boy looked up and gave a small smile. He pushed his glasses up on to the bridge of his nose. 'I think we're going to get on,' he said.

It was not long before a steady stream of pupils began to appear at Dominic's side to deposit litter into the plastic bag that he had in front of him. Nathan Thomas appeared on several occasions and took great delight in dropping into the bag assorted crisp packets, sweet wrappers, silver foil from chocolate bars, toffee papers and empty soft-drink cans. His last trip to the front of the coach, however, was for a very different reason.

'Sir,' he said to Mr Risley-Newsome, who was poring over a particularly detailed Ordnance Survey map.

'What is it?' snapped the teacher.

'I feel sick, sir.'

'What?'

'Sir, I feel sick,' Nathan repeated. 'Sir, it's really bumpy on the back seat and there's a funny smell.'

'Someone was sick all over the back seat,' explained the coach driver, without taking his eyes off the road. 'Vomit everywhere. I've cleaned it a couple of times but that sort of smell does tend to linger. I think the person had been eating very greasy fish and chips that hadn't agreed with him. Or it might have been curry. All over the place it was.'

Nathan Thomas's face turned the colour of the sick bucket a pale green.

'Sir, I really am going to be sick,' groaned Nathan.

'Dowson!' ordered Mr Risley-Newsome. 'The bucket!' He turned to Nathan Thomas. 'You sit down at the front here and you, Dowson, go and sit at the back.'

Dominic was just about to move when Miss Pruitt, who had been particularly placid and quiet so far, swivelled round on her seat.

'Mr Risley-Newsome,' she said, with a slight edge to her voice, 'Nathan Thomas happens to be one of my pupils and I shall deal with this, if you wouldn't mind. I don't think it's a very good idea at all, that Nathan should exchange places with Dominic.'

'Excuse me?'

'I said, I don't think it is a very good idea that Nathan should exchange places with Dominic.'

'You don't?' said a rather startled Mr Risley-Newsome. He was not used to being contradicted.

'No, I don't. After all, you asked Dominic to sit down at the front in order that you could keep an eye on him. It seems to me that he should not be the one to move when it is clear to me that Nathan Thomas,' she tilted her head in the direction of the panting boy, 'has been up and down the aisle of this coach like a shuttlecock, backwards and forwards, depositing all manner of sweet wrappers and crisp packets and cans and I don't know what in the litter bag. It comes as no surprise to me that he is feeling sick. He's eaten enough to stock an entire sweet shop. Give Nathan the bucket, please, Dominic. He may return to the rear of the coach with it and use it if necessary.'

'I don't mind going to the back, miss,' said Dominic cheerfully. *After all*, he thought to himself, *I wanted to be there in the first place with my two friends.*

'You stay where you are, Dominic,' said Miss Pruitt.

'Yes, miss,' he replied.

Nathan looked in the direction of the teacher appealingly but Mr Risley-Newsome grimaced and grunted and returned to studying the map. Dominic passed him the bucket and Nathan headed off to the back of the bus. Moments later various retching noises could be heard, followed by assorted 'Eeeerghs' and 'Aaaaghs' from the pupils sitting near him.

'I'm glad you didn't move,' Gerald told Dominic. 'I don't like that Nathan. I like your teacher, though. She's nice, your Miss Pruitt. I wish she taught me.'

'She's great,' said Dominic.

When the coach stopped at a large roadside cafe for its scheduled break, Dominic went in search of a bin for the litter and Nathan Thomas went in search of the toilets to dispose of the contents of the plastic bucket. They arrived back at the coach at the same time.

'Fancy one of my cheese and onion crisps?' Dominic asked him in his most innocent of voices.

Nathan's ashen face turned to the colour of a gooseberry again. The bucket was put to good use a second time.

For the remainder of the journey, Mr Risley-Newsome decided to give a running commentary on the area through which the bus travelled, describing the scenery, noting buildings of interest and pointing out unusual geographical features. He commandeered the microphone from the driver and, holding it close to his mouth, started his lecture in a deeply un-interesting voice. After five minutes of the tedious monologue, Dominic, from his vantage point on the front seat, saw the driver surreptitiously reach down below his dashboard and switch off the microphone.

Unbeknown to the teacher himself, Mr Risley-Newsome was the only one who could hear what he was saying. Miss Pruitt did not enlighten him but sat, as Dominic observed, with a small smile on her face. At the first set of traffic lights, when the coach drew to a halt, the driver turned and winked at Dominic.

It was nearly midday when the driver swung the coach into a wide, white-gravel drive. He pulled up with a jerk outside a great, rambling, grey stone house with tall mullioned windows, half obscured by dark, twisting, green ivy and the bare branches of a tall sycamore tree. It looked a cold and lonely building.

'What a dump!' exclaimed Nathan Thomas.

'Yeah, what a dump,' repeated Darren.

'It looks great!' said Dominic to Gerald.

'I like old houses,' replied his companion. 'We live in an old house with attics and cellars.'

'I wish I did,' said Dominic thoughtfully, and began another of his dreams.

Mr Risley-Newsome stood, peered out of a side window, then pivoted round to face the children. 'Remain in your seats, everyone. I shall make our presence known to the warden of the youth hostel and sort out the accommodation.' He turned to Miss Pruitt. 'You'll be all right by yourself for a minute won't you, Miss Pruitt?' he asked.

'Oh, I think I might just be able to manage, Mr Risley-Newsome,' she replied sarcastically, putting on a simpering voice.

Five minutes later the children were gathered in the large entrance hall of the house, being welcomed by Miss Brewster, the warden, a round jolly woman with a cheerful smile and friendly eyes.

'Well,' she said, 'I was getting worried. I expected you earlier.'

'We were late getting away,' the coach driver told her, glancing in the direction of Mr Risley-Newsome. 'We hit the early morning traffic.'

'Well, you're here now, safe and sound, and that's all that matters,' said Miss Brewster. 'And it's lovely to see you all. Welcome to Thundercliff Manor. I do hope that your few days with us will be really nice.' At that moment a frisky white West Highland terrier scurried into the entrance hall, yapping wildly and slipping on the polished floor. 'Stop it, Daisy!' Miss Brewster told the dog. 'She's excited, seeing all these new people.' The dog ran round in circles, its stumpy tail wagging madly.

'Is that dog dangerous?' asked Mr Risley-Newsome, retreating in the direction of the door.

'Good gracious no, she's just happy to see you all,' said Miss Brewster.

The dog, however, was not happy to see everyone there. When it caught sight of Mr Risley-Newsome scowling by the door, it stopped running around and stared blankly at him before making a noise like a distant train – a sort of low rumbling sound. It then curled its lip and displayed an impressive set of sharp teeth.

'Daisy!' said Miss Brewster, patting the fat little head. 'Behave yourself. I've never known her react like this before.'

'Really?' mouthed Mr Risley-Newsome, looking at the small growling creature as if it was something unpleasant he had discovered on the sole of his shoe. 'I should tell you that I don't like dogs so I do hope you will keep it under control.'

'She won't bother you,' said Miss Brewster. The smile had disappeared. 'And who are you, may I ask?'

'I am Mr Risley-Newsome, in charge of this party, and this is my colleague Miss Pruitt.'

'I guessed as much,' replied Miss Brewster.

'Hello, Mrs Brewster,' said Miss Pruitt brightly.

Before the warden could reply, Mr Risley-Newsome continued. 'I received all the information about the youth hostel, the various rules and requirements, which I have studied carefully, and I can assure you we will be no trouble, no trouble at all.'

'I'm sure you won't,' said Miss Brewster.

Dominic could tell by the tone of her voice and her changed expression that the warden clearly thought the very opposite. This man was obviously going to be trouble.

'I just hope the weather holds out for you,' she said, addressing Miss Pruitt. 'It's been rain, rain and more rain.'

'Yes, the weather forecast did say –' began Miss Pruitt.

'A little wet weather does not deter us, Miss

Brewster,' announced Mr Risley-Newsome pompously. 'We are here to work and not to sightsee and sunbathe.'

Miss Brewster did not reply but just stood with, what looked to Dominic, a forced smile on her face.

Mr Risley-Newsome turned to the pupils. 'Now, before I allocate you your rooms, there are one or two ground rules about your behaviour in the hostel, of which you all need to be aware.'

Miss Pruitt looked heavenwards and the coach driver sighed heavily. Dominic caught them giving Miss Brewster a knowing look.

'I have lead more school parties than there are pebbles on the beach,' continued the teacher, 'and therefore know the procedures like the nose on my face.' The children stared at his nose intently. 'Follow my instructions and we will all have a pleasant, peaceful and trouble-free few days. Do not follow my instructions and I will be after you like a cat after a mouse. I hope I make myself perfectly clear.' Everyone stared mutely.

'These are my do's and don'ts. One: boots and outdoor clothing will be left in the tack room at the back of the house at all times, except, of course, when in use. You must not, I repeat *not*, wander around the hostel in your boots. There will be no puddles and muddy footprints on the floor.

'Two: you will hear the breakfast and the dinner gong when the meals are ready. Be prompt. If you arrive late you will go without.

'Three: when you are allocated your rooms, collect your cases, make up your beds, unpack, hang your clothes up and bring your boots and outdoor coats downstairs and put them tidily in the tack room, which I mentioned earlier.

'Four: there will be no going into other people's rooms at any time. Five: lights out at nine p.m. and no talking after that.' Mr Risley-Newsome stared at the children with his sharp green eyes. 'Are there any questions?'

Miss Pruitt had maintained a carefully blank expression up to this point, but when she saw Dominic begin to raise a hand, she fixed him with a rattle-snake glare and shook her head. He lowered his hand.

'Is there anything else I need to mention, Miss Brewster?' Mr Risley-Newsome asked the warden.

'Oh, I think you've covered just about everything,' she replied. 'Well, lunch will be ready in half an hour. That should give you enough time to settle in. When you've been told what room you're in, unpacked and done all the other little jobs, come straight down, children. I've got a piping-hot meal in the oven.'

Nathan Thomas turned a brighter shade of green and disappeared out of the front door.

Unlike the pupils of St Jude's, who had been allowed by Miss Pruitt to share with their friends, the children from Cransworth Juniors had been allocated their rooms by their teacher without any discussion. When he discovered that he was a bed short for one of his pupils, Mr Risley-Newsome scowled and ran a finger down the clipboard he was holding.

'Each room has four beds in it,' explained Miss Brewster patiently. She then added, rather smugly, 'I did say that in the information I sent you.'

'That's not a problem,' said Miss Pruitt. 'We're a pupil short in one of our rooms. There's only fifteen in our party, so one of your boys can share with three of ours.' She turned to the Cransworth pupils. 'I wonder if one of you –' she began.

'Excuse me, Miss Pruitt,' said Mr Risley-Newsome, clearly remembering her earlier words about Nathan Thomas being one of *her* pupils, 'but this concerns one of *my* pupils, and I shall deal with this, if you wouldn't mind.'

As far as Dominic and his friends were concerned it could not have turned out better. They were put in a large attic room at the very top and at the back of the house, and Gerald had been picked by Mr Risley-Newsome to join them.

'I really wasn't looking forward to coming on this trip,' Gerald told his three new friends. 'Now I have a feeling it's going to be one to remember.'

Five

An Unfortunate Discovery

The attic bedroom was very much like Dominic's own bedroom at home: a plain, square room with a wardrobe, chest of drawers and bedside cabinet, except here there were four tubular, metal-framed beds with sheets, blankets and towels neatly folded on each. The view from the window could not have been more different, however. Dominic's bedroom overlooked the busy, main road – not that he looked out very often. He hadn't much interest in watching queue upon queue of noisy spluttering cars. Anyway, the glass in the window was usually edged in dirt and grime and he could hardly see out. The view from the attic window in the youth hostel was breathtaking. The grassy ground sloped gently downwards towards the cliff edge, which fell away steeply to the sandy beach and a vast, bright, silvery sea. Rocky black outcrops rose from the shimmering water like misshapen marine creatures clothed in golden seaweed, glittering wet in the sunshine. Along the coast he could see the great sweeping curve of the bay, deep black caves and high pillars of rock, where the waves crashed in a frenzy of froth and spray or curled and arched in forests of white crests.

As his three friends unpacked, talking excitedly to each other, Dominic stood at the window in a sort of dream. He imagined stately galleons with billowing sails, crimson and gold flags fluttering from the topmost masts, the captain on the poop deck peering through a telescope. He saw the pirate sloop closing in for the kill, the skull and crossbones flapping in the breeze. He saw the great puff of white smoke as the cannons roared, and heard the shouts and screams of the pirates, their cutlasses flashing in the bright sunlight. He imagined whaling boats riding the heaving ocean, full of sailors, their harpoons raised as the great white whale surfaced, spouting water and crashing towards them.

'Come on, Dom,' urged Michael, who had unpacked his case and was keen to explore the house. 'Get your things put away or you'll have "Old Grisly-Gruesome" after you.'

It was when all the beds had been made, the clothes

hung up in the wardrobe and his three friends were standing by the door, with their boots and outdoor coats ready to take down to the tack room, that Dominic discovered something was missing.

'Crikey!' he cried. 'I've forgotten my boots!'

'What?!' exclaimed Michael, Sean and Gerald together.

'My walking boots, I forgot to bring them.' Dominic flopped on to the bed and put his head in his hands. 'When I packed all my clothes and things, I couldn't get them in, so I thought I'd carry them separately and I put them behind the back door. I've forgotten to bring them. Oh, crikey! What am I going to do?'

'I don't know,' sighed Gerald, staring down at Dominic's brightly-coloured trainers. '"Old Grisly-Gruesome" is sure to notice. He always does. He's been my teacher for over a year now and he misses nothing. He's got eyes in the back of his head.'

'You could always stand behind us,' suggested Sean weakly, 'and keep out of sight.'

'He said that he would be watching me like a hungry hawk,' moaned Dominic. 'He'll see for sure. I know he will.'

'Well, we can try,' said Gerald. 'Just stay out of sight, Dominic.'

'And don't open your mouth –' said Sean.

'And draw attention to yourself,' added Michael.

'You never know,' said Sean, 'he might not notice.'

There was a loud clanging of the gong.

'We'd better go down for lunch,' said Michael, 'or we'll all be in trouble.'

The food was exactly as Miss Pruitt had said it would be. Miss Brewster brought in bowls of steaming potatoes topped with melted butter, fat juicy sausages swimming in thick, meaty gravy, delicious mounds of cauliflower cheese, all followed by generous portions of sticky treacle tart and creamy custard. For the moment, Dominic forgot about the problem with the boots and tucked in with gusto.

'What's your room like?' asked Velma, who was sitting next to Dominic.

'Great,' he replied.

'Ours is as well. We look right out over the cliffs and can see the lighthouse.'

'Just think of all the exciting things people have seen through those windows,' said Dominic thoughtfully, looking up from his treacle tart. 'All the shipwrecks and smugglers, pirates and sea battles. I'd love to live somewhere like this.'

'So would I,' sighed Velma, looking across the table. 'Miss Brewster told us that if walls could talk this house would have really interesting stories to tell. She said that it was built over two hundred years ago for the vicar and his family.'

'For just one family?' gasped Dominic. 'Crikey. All these rooms and massive gardens just for one family.'

'Well, I suppose he had loads of children and lots of butlers and maids and gardeners,' said Velma. 'Miss Brewster took us around the house and showed us some of the rooms. There's a library, morning room, dining room, parlour, billiard room and a long conservatory at the back which faces the sea. There are big kitchens downstairs and dark cellars and old attics. During the First World War it was a hospital, then it became a school and during the Second World War it was a convalescent home. It became a youth hostel about twenty years ago.'

'Do you think there's a ghost?' asked Dominic. 'There could be the ghost of the headless gardener or the vicar's little girl who fell off the cliff while she was picking flowers and was swept away by the tide, and who comes back at the dead of night looking for her parents, wandering from room to room, a-moaning and a-groaning.'

'I hope not,' Velma said, pulling a face and shivering. 'I can't stand anything that's spooky and creepy, that moans and groans.'

Almost as if on cue, the booming voice of Mr Risley-Newsome interrupted all conversation.

'Will everyone stop what you are doing for a moment, put down your cutlery and look this way. When you have finished your lunch, stacked your dishes tidily on the trolleys and wiped the tables, I want you to meet outside the entrance for the first of our visits. This afternoon we will be taking a short walk into the village of Thundercliff Bay via the church. It's a relatively gentle walk but you will need your outdoor coat, gloves, scarf, boots, clipboard and a sharp pencil. We will be walking along the clifftop, so keep your wits about you, stay on the path and behave yourselves.'

'And bring some money,' added Miss Pruitt. 'You will be able to buy a postcard to send to your parents to let them know that you have arrived safely.'

'Scenic views,' said Mr Risley-Newsome, 'and not those rude cartoon postcards.'

Sean, Michael and Gerald tried to smother their laughter, but Dominic, true to his aim to keep a low profile, looked down.

As the children gathered at the front of the youth hostel for their trip to Thundercliff Bay, Miss Brewster approached Mr Risley-Newsome, who was studying a large map which he held before him. She was carrying a heavy, black book. Dominic positioned himself with his three friends masking him, well out of the teacher's line of vision but, being of a curious nature, he was close enough to hear the conversation which followed.

'It looks like rain again,' said Miss Brewster pleasantly.

'As I said earlier, Miss Brewster, a little rain won't deter us,' replied the teacher, not looking up.

'It really does come down heavily at this time of year.'

'I'm sure it does,' murmured Mr Risley-Newsome, not really listening.

'Before you go,' said Miss Brewster, 'could I ask you to put the details of your trip in the book? I need to know where you are going and what time you are expected back.'

The teacher looked up and frowned. 'Excuse me?'

'I said, could I ask you to put the details of your trip in the book? I need to know where you are going and what time you are expected back.'

'Why?'

'Well, just in case of an emergency.'

Mr Risley-Newsome gave a little laugh. 'I don't envisage any emergency, Miss Brewster,' he told her. 'I have a great deal of experience in leading school trips and I have never had any emergencies.'

Miss Brewster sighed. 'I'm sure you haven't, but I do need to know where you are going and when you are expected back. It's a safety check and one of the requirements for all those who stay at the youth hostel, so if you wouldn't mind . . .' She held out the book.

'Very well,' sighed Mr Risley-Newsome, taking the book and scribbling in the details.

'If you are overdue for some reason,' explained the warden, 'I can contact the police. Better safe than sorry, I always say.' There was a touch of sarcasm in her next sentence. 'Of course, I am sure it's just a formality for you, being so aware as you are of safety issues and what with all your experience in leading school trips.'

'Quite,' replied Mr Risley-Newsome.

When they were ready to set off for Thundercliff Bay, Dominic sandwiched himself between Michael and Sean, with Gerald placed strategically in front, well out of the eagle eye of Mr Risley-Newsome.

The teacher, who frequently consulted his map and compass, was far more concerned with leading the crocodile of children in the right direction than bothering about Dominic and he strode ahead like Scott of the Antarctic, with Miss Pruitt bringing up the rear.

'Is he always like this?' Sean asked Gerald, as they plodded behind Mr Risley-Newsome. He wished he had never asked.

Gerald, who had been extremely quiet and shy when they had first met him, suddenly launched into a long and detailed account and there was no stopping him.

'Oh, yes,' he said, nodding vigorously. 'Once he made all the class stand out in the playground in the freezing cold because somebody had talked on the way into school. And another time he tore pages out of everyone's books because the writing wasn't neat enough. When he marks your work he uses a really thick felt-tip pen and covers your page in red. It looks as if he's bled all over it. I hate handing work in to him. It comes back full of all sorts of comments. And at lunchtimes you're not allowed to leave anything on your plate. You can't get up from the table until everything is eaten.'

'Do you –' began Sean.

'The worst thing about him, though,' continued Gerald, without seeming to take a breath, 'is he's never wrong. Once he told us the biggest dinosaur that ever lived was a diplodocus. I know a lot about dinosaurs. I've got loads of books about them. Anyway, I told Risley-Newsome it was the brachiosaurus. Actually, the diplodocus was the longest, it was about twenty-six metres, longer than two buses standing end to end. But the brachiosaurus was twelve metres tall, which is taller than two giraffes. It weighed thirty tonnes and was as heavy as eight elephants. My favourite dinosaur is the deinonychus. It was really small but it had huge slashing claws and –'

'Wow!' interrupted Dominic. 'You do know a lot about dinosaurs.'

'I know,' said Gerald, keen to continue. 'Anyway, Mr Risley-Newsome wouldn't have it, even when I tried to show him where it was written in the book. He said the book must have got it wrong. You soon learn to say nothing and you never ever argue with him.' Gerald paused. Dominic was quick to take the opportunity of getting a word in.

'I don't know why he ever became a teacher,' Dominic said. 'He doesn't sound as if he likes kids.'

'He became a teacher,' observed Michael, 'because he likes ordering people about. That's what teachers like to do – order you about.'

'Your mum's a teacher,' said Dominic.

'I know, and *she* likes ordering people about as well. She orders my dad about, she orders my sister about and she orders me about. She can't help it. It's not really her fault. You see, when they're at college training to be teachers they have special classes telling them how to order people about.'

Dominic thought for a moment. 'I bet "Old Grisly-Gruesome" came top of that class,' he said.

Six

The Legend of Reverend Bentley-Brewster

Their first stop was the church – a square, squat, grey building enclosed by red, rusting iron railings. It stood on a small knoll set back from the cliff edge and above the village. Several thick stone steps, green with lichen, led to the gate, and beyond a narrow path wound its way like a snake through the graveyard and thick shaggy grass to the church's porch. To the front of the church was an overgrown wooded area, choked with nettles and thistles, ancient bushes, sharp and twisted like barbed wire, and stunted, uprooted trunks, like a mass of huge, petrified claws. The air was full of the smell of salt and ivy, wild garlic and rotting wood. The iron gate creaked open crookedly on one hinge as the teachers and pupils made their way to the porch. The graveyard was full of tombstones, some in dark shiny granite, others in pearly white marble, some in greasy grey slate, others in pitted sandstone. They had been mostly forgotten, cracked and broken, ribboned with creepers or moss-covered. Some were strewn with dead flowers, shrivelled and black.

'It's really spooky,' whispered Velma to Dominic.

'I bet "Old Grisly-Gruesome" feels really at home here,' he replied.

The heavy door of the church was made of carved oak with shallow panels sunk in bevelled frames. Mr Risley-Newsome rattled the great iron ring noisily.

'Unfortunately it's locked,' he said, turning to the children gathered round him. 'It looks as if the church study will have to be delayed for the time being.'

'May I try?' asked Miss Pruitt and, not waiting for an answer, slid past him and gently turned the iron ring, which gave easily. The door swung open.

Dominic expected the interior of the church to be dark and musty and cold. It was, however, warm and welcoming, and smelt surprisingly fresh and pleasant. Rows of highly-polished pews faced the chancel and high altar and four vivid stained-glass windows, each depicting different seascapes, were cut into the thick stone walls. In the centre of the church was a huge, polished, brass lectern in the shape of an eagle, its out-spread wings supporting a large bible. With its sharp beak and fierce, staring eyes, Dominic thought it bore a remarkable resemblance to Mr Risley-Newsome. He stared up at the great, golden bird.

'Now, don't touch anything,' commanded Mr Risley-Newsome, looking in Dominic's direction. Dominic had positioned himself behind a pew so his trainers could not be seen. 'We do not want the vicar arriving to find a broken statue or a damaged hymn book awaiting him. And stay away from that lectern, Dowson, it looks decidedly unsteady.'

'May I help you?' The voice came from the side of the altar. A cheerful-looking woman, rosy-cheeked, with hair tumbling over her shoulders, and her hands full of bright flowers and ferns, emerged from the shadows.

'Ah,' said Mr Risley-Newsome. 'Would it be at all possible for us to have a look around the church, as part of our studies? We are on a school trip and staying at the youth hostel.'

'Of course,' replied the woman. 'If you like, I could give you a guided tour. I'm only here this afternoon to arrange the flowers for tomorrow's service. I don't have anything else on.'

'That would be nice,' said Miss Pruitt. 'Lovely flowers.'

'Yes, they are,' agreed the woman. 'I do think flowers brighten up the church, particularly at this time of year.'

'Do you think we ought to get the permission of the vicar?' asked Mr Risley-Newsome. 'I know how difficult some of these clergymen can be when it comes to groups of children wandering around their church.'

'No, not at all,' replied the woman pleasantly, putting the flowers down on a table. 'The vicar loves to have children in the church.'

'Nevertheless,' said Mr Risley-Newsome, 'I do feel we should ask him. He might not approve of a school party invading his premises.'

'I am the vicar,' said the woman simply. 'And I should be delighted to show you around the church.'

'Oh, I see,' said Mr Risley-Newsome.

Dominic noticed that small, smug smile appearing again on Miss Pruitt's lips.

The vicar, followed by the teachers and children, toured the building, explaining that it was not one of Britain's very oldest churches, had a fairly ordinary history and was not particularly beautiful, but it was small and homely and well used by the local people.

'There is one quite interesting story associated with the church, though,' she told the children when they had gathered beneath a small brass plate set high in the wall. 'I'll just give you a few moments to read what is written,' she said, pointing to the plaque. It read:

In memory of the Reverend Joseph Elias Bentley-Brewster, who departed this earthly life on the 20th day of March, 1799. He was a dearly loved husband, father and servant of Christ. His natural temper was affable and his conversation pleasing and prudent. His life was exemplary and regular and consistent with his chosen vocation as a priest.

'Now, the Reverend Bentley-Brewster was rector here over two hundred years ago, and a bit of a character by all accounts,' said the vicar. 'He lived up in the big house which is now the youth hostel where you are all staying.'

'Miss, he might have been related to Miss Brewster, who runs the youth hostel,' said Dominic excitedly.

'Brewster is a very common name,' said Mr Risley-Newsome, dismissively. 'Now, let the vicar continue, and listen.'

Michael and Sean pulled faces in Dominic's direction and mouthed: 'Shut up!'

'I thought he was keeping a low profile,' whispered Gerald. 'He's drawing attention to himself again.'

Sean sighed. 'He can't help it.'

'That's Dominic's trouble,' said Michael, 'he just can't help himself.'

'It's an interesting thought about the name,' said the vicar. 'Miss Brewster might indeed be a long-lost descendant of quite a famous man. He did have a lot of children by all accounts. There are quite a lot of Brewsters who live hereabouts.'

'Why was he famous?' asked Velma.

'Well,' said the vicar, lowering her voice, 'the Reverend Joseph Bentley-Brewster, so they say, was a smuggler in his spare time.'

'A smuggler!' gasped Dominic.

'He and a group of local men were reputed to have hidden casks of brandy and barrels of wine in the caves below the cliffs.'

'Were they ever caught?' asked Sean Murphy.

'No, never, although, so the story goes, the Reverend Bentley-Brewster was suspected and questioned by the customs men, who looked high and low for the contraband. I am sure they had a sneaking suspicion that he was involved in smuggling, but they never caught him. They searched the church and the crypt, the house and its cellars and could never find so much as a bottle. Many was the time when the customs men watched from the clifftop when the smugglers were rowing ashore. They saw them land in the little cove just below the vicarage and unload all the cargo.'

'Why didn't they go down on the beach to get them?' asked Michael.

'Because that little cove has two sharp headlands jutting out on either side,' the vicar told them. 'The cliffs curve out like the horns of a bull and cut the cove off when the tide is in. The cliffs are steep and slippery there, so it was no use the customs men trying to climb down. They'd have got stuck in the mud. They just had to wait on the clifftop, watching helplessly as the smugglers brought all the barrels and casks ashore. Then, when the tide turned, they made their way along the beach at Thundercliff Bay. Of course, when they arrived at the cove there was no sign of anybody or anything. It was as if the smugglers had disappeared into thin air. They searched the caves with a fine toothcomb but found nothing. There must have been some sort of hidden chamber in the caves or secret passage leading up to the village.'

'So, somewhere there could be all this treasure,' gasped Dominic. 'Hidden away.'

'I think, somehow, it would have been discovered by now,' smiled the vicar.

'Yes, indeed,' remarked Mr Risley-Newsome. 'All very interesting, I am sure, but it seems to me that his epitaph does not describe the Reverend Bentley-Brewster very accurately. I should hardly say that the illegal activities of this man could be "exemplary and regular and consistent with his chosen profession as a priest", if indeed he was a thief.'

'Well, perhaps "thief" is a rather strong word to use. He was a smuggler and he never profited from his smuggling,' said the vicar gently. 'He was a sort of Robin Hood figure by all accounts. He died without a penny to his name. So the story goes, he gave all the money he made from smuggling to the poor and needy, and in those days there were a great many destitute people.'

'That hardly excuses criminal behaviour,' said Mr Risley-Newsome pompously. 'And as for being famous, I should say "infamous" is a more fitting description of the man.'

Dominic could see by the expression on the vicar's face that she joined the many in taking a dislike to the teacher. She managed, however, to remain pleasant.

'Are there any more questions?' she asked.

'Miss, did they ever find a secret cave or hidden passage?' asked Dominic.

'No, but then it's only a story and there probably was no secret cave or hidden passage.'

'Probably a cock-and-bull story,' remarked Mr Risley-Newsome, consulting his watch. 'A lot of these tales are not based on fact but just made up for the tourists. They were invented by people with over-active imaginations. Well, we must move on. Thank you for the tour, Vicar. Very enlightening. Follow me, everybody, and don't dawdle behind. The next stop is Thundercliff Bay, and remember what I said about the postcards.' With that he strode for the door.

'Thank you so much,' said Miss Pruitt to the vicar. 'It was very good of you to take the time and the trouble to show us around your lovely church.'

'My pleasure,' replied the vicar, shaking her head and thinking to herself how very different teachers could be.

Dominic was unusually quiet as they set off for Thundercliff Bay. His mind was full of exciting thoughts. *Suppose there is a secret passage leading up from the beach to the house, a hidden room full of smugglers' booty, chests of golden coins, cutlasses and muskets, barrels of brandy and bottles of rum. It could be behind a secret panel, maybe in the library, or beneath a flagstone in the kitchen. There might be a passageway behind the fireplace. It would be dark and musty and covered with centuries of cobwebs. There might be the skeleton of a smuggler, there might be . . .*

'Dominic Dowson!' It was Mr Risley-Newsome breaking into his thoughts in that unpleasantly loud and strident voice.

Dominic nearly jumped out of his trainers. 'Yes, sir?' he cried. *Now I'm in for it*, he thought. He should have stayed hidden in the cluster of pupils, away from the eagle eyes of the teacher. So lost had he been in his thoughts about smugglers and hidden treasure that he had wandered away from his friends and from the path.

'Come here!' ordered Mr Risley-Newsome.

Dominic made his way through the pupils until he was standing in front of the teacher. 'Yes, sir?'

'What did I say before we set off?'

'You said we would need our outdoor coats, gloves, scarves and . . . boots,' said the boy quietly.

'What else did I say?' He waited for a reply but Dominic just held his head down and felt it best to say nothing. 'Did I or did I not say to stay on the path?'

'Yes, sir.'

'Then why are you not on the path?'

'I don't know, sir,' said Dominic.

'You are not on the path because you do not listen! Now, keep your mind on what you are doing, Dominic Dowson, and stop daydreaming. These cliffs are dangerous. The last thing we want is some silly boy falling off them.'

'Yes, sir,' he replied, with a great inward sigh of relief. 'Old Grisly-Gruesome' hadn't noticed his trainers. Dominic edged his way through the pupils and took up a position right at the back, next to Velma. He hadn't been aware, until it was too late, that Nathan Thomas and Darren Wilmott were also at the back.

Seven

The Rock Bun Incident

Thundercliff Bay was little more than a higgledy-piggledy cluster of brightly-painted houses and cottages hugging the cliff side. Narrow, pale-blue and green rendered buildings were sandwiched between larger stone villas and red-bricked terraces, and all were linked by a labyrinth of narrow alleys and cobbled snickleways. There was a run-down inn – the 'Three Jolly Smugglers' – a cafe – 'The Rumbling Tum' – a squat Seaman's Mission and a general store-cum-post-office-cum-gift-shop. And that was just about it.

'What a dump,' muttered Nathan, as the line of

73

children meandered slowly between the houses.

'Yeah, what a dump,' agreed Darren, nodding vigorously.

'There's more life in a deserted cemetery,' continued Nathan. 'Come to Thundercliff Bay and die. It's a dead hole. There's nothing here. No fish and chip shops, no arcades, no amusements, no proper shops. Nothing.'

'It's a dump,' said Darren, 'a real dump.'

'I've just said it was a dump!' snapped Nathan irritably.

'Oh, yeah,' said Darren, giving his companion a weak smile.

'I wish I was at home,' sighed Nathan, blowing out a mouthful of air dramatically. 'At home in my own bedroom in front of my computer, where it's warm. I'm freezing cold, bored and fed up.'

'Yeah, so am I,' agreed Darren.

'Tramping up and down in a boring place, all wet and cold and hungry and bored.' He caught sight of Dominic, striding out ahead of him. 'I bet Dowson likes it.'

'I do, as a matter of fact,' said Dominic. 'It's really interesting.'

'It would be for you,' laughed Nathan.

'Yeah, it would be for you,' echoed Darren.

'You've probably never been further than the bottom of your street,' said Nathan. 'I've been to Disneyworld, Majorca, Tenerife, Florida –'

'Oh, do shut up, Nathan Thomas!' snapped Miss

Pruitt suddenly. She had been following up the rear to chivvy stragglers but close enough to hear his complaining. 'You have done nothing but moan and groan since you got on the coach at school, except for the occasion when you had your head in the plastic bucket and that was the result of stuffing yourself silly with sweets and crisps and all manner of things. And as for being at home in your nice warm bedroom in front of your computer, you wouldn't be there at this time of day, would you? You'd be back at school in the classroom, making clever comments, no doubt.'

'Wow,' whispered Velma to Dominic. 'That's telling him. Your teacher can be really snappy, can't she?'

'She's not like that normally,' Dominic told her. 'She's usually very nice and friendly.'

'I bet it's Mr Risley-Newsome who's put her in a bad mood,' Velma told him. 'I heard them talking at lunch and he went on and on about how he had taken ages to arrange all the trips and find all the information, plan the routes and decide where we would be going and what we would be seeing. She was just about to take a sip of her coffee when he told her that caffeine was bad for her. When she reached for the butter he told her it was fattening and full of cholesterol and that margarine was healthier for her. Then, just before we were setting off, he told her she needed a proper anorak and proper walking boots.'

'Mr Know-It-All,' said Dominic.

'Well, I'm bored, miss.' Nathan was still grumbling. 'There's nothing to do.'

'You want to count yourself lucky,' Miss Pruitt told him. 'There's many a boy would like to have a healthy walk at the seaside instead of sitting at a desk in a stuffy classroom on a Monday afternoon.'

'I *do* like the seaside, miss,' said Nathan. 'It's just that I don't like this particular seaside.'

He should have had the good sense, thought Dominic, as he listened to the boy's whining tones, *to shut up*. Dominic's gran used to tell him that if you ever get in a hole, stop digging.

Nathan continued to shovel away regardless. 'We go to Majorca and the Canary Islands and Spain and Florida for our holidays,' he told Miss Pruitt and any-one else prepared to listen. 'That's the sort of seaside I like, where it's hot and you can go in the sea. There's lots to do. I'd sooner be there than here.'

'And I would sooner you were there than here, as well,' said Miss Pruitt. 'In fact, I would sooner you were anywhere, so I don't have to listen to your constant carping and complaining. Go and join Mr Risley-Newsome at the front and see how he likes your grousing and grumbling. Go on. Because I'm fed up with hearing your voice.'

'It's all right, miss,' said Nathan quickly. The thought of having to spend the next few miles next to Mr Risley-Newsome and endure his do's and don'ts was not a pleasant prospect.

'No, Nathan,' replied Miss Pruitt smartly. 'It is not

76

all right. Go on, get yourself down to the front and take Darren with you. I am weary of hearing that whining, whinging voice of yours. Go on and give me a bit of peace and quiet.'

The two boys slouched off. The two pupils who were now in front of the teacher were Dominic and Velma.

'And how about you, Dominic?' asked Miss Pruitt. 'Do you find it boring?'

'No, miss!' exclaimed Dominic. 'It's fantastic.'

'Well,' said the teacher, a wry smile playing on her lips, 'I wouldn't go quite that far. Interesting possibly, but fantastic is something of an exaggeration.'

'I've only been to the seaside once, miss,' Dominic was telling her cheerfully as he breathed in the fresh salty air. 'I went to Blackpool in a caravan with my mum and my gran. We had a great time on the Pleasure Beach, up the tower, on the donkeys. Gran bought a hat with "Kiss Me Quick!" on and this pensioner followed her all down the pier. I had this massive ice cream with fruit and cherries and nuts. It was called a "Knickerbocker Glory". We had a really good time.' He paused. 'But we did have a bit of bother in Blackpool, miss.'

Miss Pruitt sighed. 'A bit of bother? What bit of bother would this be?'

'I know what you're thinking, miss,' said Dominic, giving her a cheeky grin, 'but it really wasn't my fault.'

'It never is, Dominic,' said Miss Pruitt, recalling the fiasco with the paint. 'It never is.'

'So, what happened?' asked Velma.

'It was all the fault of this stupid seagull,' Dominic explained.

'A seagull,' chuckled Miss Pruitt. 'Now, that is an original excuse. Whatever did the seagull do?'

'Well, miss, it was like this. My mum and my gran decided to go on the pier for a cup of tea. I got Gran her tea and a cake from the cafe. It was actually a bun, called a rock bun, and it was really hard like a rock, as well. Gran (she has false teeth you see) couldn't bite into it, so she gave it to me. Well, it was horrible, seriously horrible, all stale and dry and taste-less like crunchy cardboard. Gran told me to throw it to the seagulls, so I did.'

'Well, that doesn't sound too disastrous to me,' said Miss Pruitt.

'So I threw this rock bun, which was hard as iron, off the pier and it shot out of my hand like a cannon-ball and it hit this low-flying seagull. It knocked it clean out of the sky.'

'You hit a seagull!' cried Velma.

'I didn't mean to do it, it was an accident, a fluke accident. It just happened to be in the wrong place at the wrong time.'

'How many times have I heard that, Dominic?' Miss Pruitt murmured.

'Anyway this seagull went all wobbly, gave a sort of pathetic squawk and then plummeted into the sea with a big *kerploosh!*'

'Was it all right?' asked Miss Pruitt.

'Oh, yes, miss, it just looked a bit dazed.'

'Well, no real harm was done, then,' said the teacher.

'Yes, there was, miss,' Dominic told her, nodding. 'You see, the rock bun sort of ricocheted off the sea-gull, like a boomerang. It was picked up by the strong wind and blown back on to the pier and that's when it hit this old woman.'

'There was a woman?' sighed Miss Pruitt, pulling a pained expression.

'Sitting on the pier having a cup of tea.'

'And the rock bun hit her?'

'Yes, miss, smack in the middle of her head. She was very shocked.'

'I imagine she was,' remarked the teacher, attempting to stop herself from smiling.

'And she dropped her cup of tea and –'

'And it scalded her,' said Miss Pruitt.

'Oh, no, miss, she was all right.'

'Well, thank heaven for small mercies.'

'It was the dog that it scalded.'

'There was a dog?' sighed Miss Pruitt, her bad mood disappearing fast.

'A chihuahua sitting under the table. You can imagine how startled it was, having a hot cup of tea spilt all over it.'

Miss Pruitt pictured the mayhem. 'I can indeed,' she said, trying to suppress her laughter.

'It sort of jumped up, yelped like mad, ran off and that's when it ended up in the water.'

'It fell off the pier?' gasped Velma.

'Not exactly fell, sort of leapt.'

'The trouble you cause, Dominic,' said Miss Pruitt, shaking her head. 'Trouble is your middle name.'

'It wasn't my fault, miss. It was the seagull's.'

'So, what happened to the dog?' asked Velma, fascinated by the account.

'Well, this old woman went bananas, jumping up and down and screaming and shouting and waving her arms about. It was lucky the tide was in and the pier wasn't too high, otherwise the dog could have got hurt.'

'So, the dog was all right?' asked Velma.

'Oh, yes, and as my gran explained to this woman, it probably enjoyed its little swim and, in any case, people shouldn't bring animals on the pier because if they do they are asking for trouble.'

'She sounds quite a character, your grandma, Dominic,' said Miss Pruitt.

'She is, miss.'

Miss Pruitt certainly felt a whole lot brighter. She had to hand it to the boy. He was an interesting character, troublesome maybe, full of mischief, accident-prone certainly, but good-hearted and easy to please. He never complained, tried to be helpful and was always cheerful, except when in trouble and then he would look up with those doleful eyes and make you feel sorry for him. What's more, he could tell a very entertaining story. *He has a wild and wonderful imagination has Dominic Dowson*, she thought to herself, smiling. It was the first smile she had had that day.

'I think you had better stay clear of seagulls and rock buns on this trip, Dominic,' said Miss Pruitt, chuckling.

Mr Risley-Newsome's loud and penetrating voice shattered the happy atmosphere at the rear of the group. Ordering everyone to stop and gather round him, he commenced another lecture on the do's and don'ts. With bored faces, the children formed a half-circle round the teacher, who consulted his watch theatrically.

'Right. Now, before I let you visit the shop there are one or two ground rules of which you need to be aware.'

Miss Pruitt gazed heavenwards and sighed inwardly, her good mood having instantly vanished.

'One: you have ten minutes, and ten minutes only, to purchase a postcard to send home and, if you wish, a small present for your parents.

'Two: you are not to buy sticky rock, fizzy drinks, crisps, sweets or cheap plastic toys.

'Three: make certain you pay for everything. Anyone who feels inclined to be light-fingered –'

Miss Pruitt, who had clearly had enough, threaded her way swiftly though the throng of children. 'Mr Risley-Newsome,' she said in an undertone and trying to suppress her anger, 'there is really no necessity to warn any of *my* pupils about shoplifting. I can assure you that none of my children is a thief.'

'Excuse me?'

'I said,' repeated Miss Pruitt slowly, 'that there is no need to warn any of *my* pupils about shoplifting.'

Mr Risley-Newsome was entirely unabashed by Miss Pruitt's sharp interruption and, speaking in a voice loud enough for all the children to hear, remarked: 'I have always been of the opinion that it is best to be perfectly clear from the outset about such things. It is easy to be wise after the event.' He continued undeterred. 'Four: we will assemble, after you have looked around the shop, in an orderly fashion outside "The Rumbling Tum" cafe. Be careful, be sensible and be back on time. You may go.'

As the pupils dispersed, Miss Pruitt took a deep breath and turned to her colleague, who was consulting his map. Dominic sat on a nearby step to tie his shoelace and, accidentally on purpose, overheard their heated conversation. He had not fully realized until the start of the trip that teachers, like pupils, sometimes do not get on. They, too, have their differences and disagreements, as he soon found out. As Mr Merriman might say, Miss Pruitt now 'had the bit between her teeth'.

'Mr Risley-Newsome,' she said, controlling her anger, 'would it be possible for you to consult me occasionally before making decisions. Since the start of this trip you have organized everything. I sometimes feel like one of the pupils rather than a colleague teacher. This is supposed to be a joint venture.'

She is right, thought Dominic. *He has taken charge*

of everything. Do this, do that, don't do this, don't do that.

'Miss Pruitt,' replied Mr Risley-Newsome, producing his patronizing smile, 'I think that you would be the first to admit that I have infinitely more experience in leading school trips than you. Over the years, I have taken children on coaches and trains, boats and planes and I am fully qualified in outdoor pursuits, orienteering, mountain rescue, first aid and survival techniques. I cannot see the point in constantly consulting you as to what to do. It is time-consuming for me and confusing for the children.'

'I am well aware of your many qualifications and your extensive experience, Mr Risley-Newsome,' replied Miss Pruitt, refusing to be put off. 'Nevertheless, I would like, at the very least, to be informed as to what you have planned. You have organized the whole week, devised the itinerary, decided on the programme, produced the worksheets, dealt with room allocations – just about everything.'

Dominic had never seen this side of his teacher before. The calm, friendly, easy-going, cheerful Miss Pruitt had suddenly changed into this angry, stubborn and bad-tempered woman with a face like thunder. It was a bit like his gran and the incident with the seagull. She had been fine until the woman had started calling her grandson names. Then Gran had really told the woman with the chihuahua what was what.

'Miss Pruitt,' replied Mr Risley-Newsome, 'let me make one thing clear.' The patronizing smile had disappeared. 'The only reason our two schools are on a joint trip is that there was no available woman member of staff at Cransworth to accompany me. Otherwise –'

'I am perfectly aware of that,' replied Miss Pruitt. 'I would ask you, however, that in future you do me the courtesy of consulting me before you make any decisions concerning *my* pupils.' Without waiting for a reply, she walked briskly away with her head in the air.

Mr Risley-Newsome caught sight of Dominic, wide-eyed and open-mouthed, sitting on the step. 'And what are you doing there, Dowson?'

'Tying my shoelace, sir,' Dominic replied.

'Then tie it!' he snapped, before also walking briskly away with *his* head in the air.

So much for having eyes like an eagle, thought Dominic, smiling. 'Old Grisly-Gruesome' hadn't even noticed his trainers.

Eight

The Mystery of the Hidden Treasure

On the way back to the youth hostel along the clifftop, Mr Risley-Newsome struck off ahead with a powerful, determined tread. He was too wrapped up in his own thoughts to notice the boy in the brightly-coloured trainers trying to keep out of sight.

'Come along! Come along!' he shouted irritably to the children panting and puffing behind him. 'Keep up! It's like leading a lot of geriatric tortoises.'

'He never even noticed my trainers,' Dominic told his friends excitedly. 'They were staring him in the face. I was sitting there on this step, tying my shoelace, and he looked straight at them and never said a word.'

'Doesn't sound like Mr Risley-Newsome,' said Gerald. 'He must have something on his mind. He never misses a trick usually.'

'Well, he missed my trainers,' said Dominic, 'and that's all I'm bothered about. In the words of my head-teacher: "I'm home and dry" and "safe as houses".'

Later that evening, after a dinner of thick, meaty stew with rich gravy, huge dumplings, creamy potatoes and fresh vegetables, followed by home-made apple pie and cream, Dominic's table was assigned to help Miss Brewster with the washing-up.

'I never wash up at home,' announced Nathan, carrying a pile of plates to the sink.

'I never do, either,' echoed Darren.

'Well, now is your chance to learn,' Miss Brewster told him cheerfully. 'Put them in the sink and get washing.'

'We've got a dishwasher at home,' Nathan told her and anyone who would listen, 'and we have a cleaning woman who comes in twice a week to clean the house.'

'My goodness,' said the warden. 'I didn't know we'd got royalty staying with us. I should have put down the red carpet and got out my best china.'

'Actually, we've got a red carpet in our lounge,' announced Nathan.

'We've got one on our stairs,' said Darren.

Miss Brewster smiled and shook her head, thinking to herself how very different children could be.

When all the cups and saucers and plates had been dried and stacked, the cutlery put away and the surfaces wiped down, the pupils headed for the games room to watch television. Dominic and Velma remained behind. They had something to ask the warden.

'Miss Brewster?' said Dominic, casually folding up a tea towel.

'Yes, love.'

'Are you related to the man in the church?'

'And which man would that be?'

'The smuggler, Joseph Bentley-Brewster.'

'And who told you about Joseph Bentley-Brewster?'

'The vicar told us,' said Velma. 'We visited the church today and she showed us around.'

'There are lots of Brewsters in these parts,' said the warden.

'That's what the vicar told us,' said Velma.

'And did she also tell you that her name is Brewster?'

'No,' said Dominic.

'Well, it is. She's my niece.'

'So, you both could be descended from Joseph Bentley-Brewster,' said Dominic. 'Wow!'

'Well, I'll tell you this: we would both like to think that he was one of our ancestors. He was a very good man by all accounts was the Reverend Joseph Bentley-Brewster, a very kind and gentle man, and he did a lot for the poor and needy. Many is the family he saved from starvation.'

'And he was a smuggler?'

'So they say, but it could just be an old tale. Certainly there were men from the village who brought over from Holland silks and laces, bottles of rum and casks of brandy and they say the customs men never found so much as a box of nails.'

'Where did they hide it all?' asked Dominic.

'There's the mystery. Nobody really knows. Probably deep down in the caves by the seashore, I should imagine. There's a whole network of tunnels and passages leading into the cliff. People have searched for a hidden cave, of course – potholers and climbers; people with metal detectors – but nothing's ever been found. If there was a secret cave, the smugglers took the secret to their graves.'

'So nobody's found the treasure?' asked Dominic.

'Goodness me, there was no treasure, love!' exclaimed Miss Brewster. 'If the Reverend Bentley-Brewster was a smuggler, as people say, then he gave it all away. He died with not a penny to his name.'

'He might have kept some hidden in a secret room in this house,' said Dominic, rather disappointed.

'I think by this time it would have been discovered, don't you? When they used the house during the war as a convalescent home, it was knocked about a bit by the soldiers and no mistake. Then, when it became a school, they had to knock walls down, turn rooms into classrooms and replace all the electrics and the plumbing. They would surely have found any secret passages or hidden rooms then, don't you think? I've been in this house for twenty years and I know every inch of the place. No, there's no hidden treasure behind the walls.'

'Are there any ghosts, Miss Brewster?' asked Velma.

'No, there are no ghosts here, either.'

'I'm glad about that,' sighed Velma.

'But not too far from here, at Brandon Bridge, there is the "Phantom Horseman",' said Miss Brewster.

'Who?' gasped Dominic.

'Pull up a chair, you two,' said the warden, 'and I'll tell you all about him.'

Later that evening everyone assembled in the lounge area for one of Mr Risley-Newsome's marathon monologues about the walk they were to undertake the following day.

'Tomorrow we will be walking firstly to Fyling-thorpe,' Mr Risley-Newsome told the children, 'which is a couple of miles or so. Make sure you are all appropriately equipped with anorak, scarf, gloves, waterproofs and boots, and have your clipboards and a sharp pencil. After Fylingthorpe we will be following the track of the old Scarborough-to-Whitby railway line. This railway line was opened in 1885 but the track is now a walkway. The old railway path continues past a place called Fylings Park, and it is interesting to note that there was probably a medieval deer park here at one time.'

The children did not look the slightest bit interested in this snippet of information and continued to stare at him with weary expressions.

'This is seriously boring,' whispered Dominic behind his hand to Gerald. 'I've got a really good story about the "Phantom Horseman". I'll tell you later, after lights out.'

'Is there something you wish to share with us, Dominic Dowson?' asked Mr Risley-Newsome.

'No, sir,' replied Dominic, putting on his most angelic expression.

'Then kindly keep your mouth closed and listen. You might just learn something.'

'Yes, sir.'

'Now, as I was saying, after Fylings Park, next stop will be Boggle Hole.' The children giggled. 'There is nothing funny about Boggle Hole,' said Mr Risley-Newsome. 'The word "boggle" is a local name for a hob or goblin, which is a mischievous elf. These mythical creatures were supposed to have lived here. It is another piece of superstitious nonsense.'

Typical, thought Dominic. *Just as it is getting interesting, he goes and changes the subject.*

'If the tide is out,' continued the teacher, 'we will walk along the shore via Robin Hoods Bay. If the tide is in we will cross the footbridge and follow the clifftop path back to the youth hostel. Are there any questions?'

'Sir,' asked Nathan, 'is Robin Hoods Bay where Robin Hood lived?'

'No, nothing of the sort. There is no evidence whatsoever that the outlaw of Sherwood Forest, if indeed he ever existed at all, came to the village. It is another piece of fiction.'

'Were there smugglers at Robin Hoods Bay, sir, like at Thundercliff Bay?' asked Dominic.

'I have no doubt that Robin Hoods Bay has had its share of thieves, looters, vagabonds and criminals, but that is of no interest to us. We will be looking at the geography of the area and not concerning ourselves with tall tales. Anyway, if we do visit Robin Hoods Bay, it will only be to pass through. We will not have time to linger there. That is not on my itinerary.'

Dominic could see that Mr Risley-Newsome had no intention of doing what Miss Pruitt had asked – to consult her. He watched her as she gave the teacher a stare that would turn milk sour.

Later that night, when the lights had been turned off, when everything was still and silent and everyone was tucked up sleeping, three boys climbed from their beds in the large attic room at the very top and at the back of the house, to hear the story of the 'Phantom Horseman of Brandon Bridge'.

'It was in the year eighteen hundred and fifty-five,' began Dominic in a hushed voice, 'when Sir Brandon de Blunderville galloped out of Greaseborough Grange on his great grey horse. He wore a coat as red as fresh blood, a top hat as black as night, and spurs as sharp and shiny as silver knives. It was a cold, cold morning and the frost covered the ground like icing sugar. Sir Brandon was off to join the hunt and chase the fox.'

'I like foxes,' said Gerald.

'Shush,' said Michael. 'Go on, Dom.'

'*Clip-clop, clip-clop* went the horse's hoofs on the frozen ground,' continued Dominic. 'Over walls he jumped, through streams, across fields, down mossy banks, after the fox. He was a cruel man was Sir Brandon and no fox had ever escaped him. On and on he rode, his sweating horse beneath him panting and blowing out clouds of steam in the cold air –'

'You're really good at telling stories, Dominic,' remarked Gerald. He didn't sound all that happy.

'Shush,' said Sean. 'Go on, Dom.'

'Then he saw it!'

'What?' gasped Gerald.

'The fox,' said Dominic. 'It was on the railway line in front of a tunnel, looking up at Sir Brandon. "Got you!" he cried, and blew his horn for the hounds. Down the bank came the dogs, leaping and springing, snarling and snapping.'

A distant owl hooted and the wind rustled the trees outside the window.

Gerald shuddered. 'This is really spooky,' he whispered.

'Shush,' said Michael. 'Go on, Dom.'

'The fox looked up for a moment and then trotted into the tunnel. None of the hounds would follow. They barked and growled and ran round in circles, but they would not go into the tunnel. Sir Brandon shouted and blew on his horn, but not a dog would go in after the fox. He dug his spurs deeply into the horse's side, leapt down the bank and galloped into the tunnel's darkness after the fox.'

'And?' asked Michael, his eyes as round as saucers.

'A train was coming from the other end.'

'Oh, heck!' murmured Gerald.

'There was a sickening thud,' continued Dominic, 'a terrible shriek of the whistle, a screeching of brakes and a scream – a terrible, eerie, frightening scream which echoed down the tunnel. Then the train appeared through great clouds of steam and thundered on down the track. The hounds ran off, yelping and whining. And do you know what?'

'What?' asked Gerald in a small voice.

'The fox came out of the tunnel, smiling,' said Dominic.

'A fox can't smile,' said Michael.

'This one did,' said Dominic. 'Sir Brandon was never seen again, but on some days when it's cold and misty and the sky is full of dark clouds, out of the tunnel gallops the "Phantom Horseman", his face as white as the sheet on my bed, his body all mangled and twisted, his eyes glowing like burning coals.' Nobody spoke. 'Are you all right, Gerald?' asked Dominic.

'No, I'm not,' he replied.

'I must admit,' said Dominic cheerfully, 'I am pretty good at telling stories. 'Night everybody.'

The next morning was cold and bright. The children assembled in front of the youth hostel. Dominic positioned himself judiciously behind his friends, well out of sight of 'Old Grisly-Gruésome'. The man in question stood shielding his eyes with a gloved hand. He looked like the leader of some great expedition in his large, green, canvas anorak with the fur-lined hood, huge, brown hiking boots, thick woollen hat, and heavy rucksack. He consulted his watch and then his compass.

'I didn't get a wink of sleep last night,' said Gerald. 'I kept thinking about that ghostly huntsman galloping out of the tunnel. And today we've got this long walk ahead of us. I could go back to bed, I'm so tired.'

'Just look at "Old Grisly-Gruesome",' said Michael.

'He looks as if he's about to climb Everest,' said Dominic.

'What was that, Dominic?' asked Miss Pruitt, who had suddenly appeared behind him.

'I said, will we ever have a rest, miss,' he replied.

'I'm sure you did,' she replied, chuckling.

'Forwards and onwards!' Mr Risley-Newsome shouted, gesturing ahead of him with a sweep of the arm, and the school party was off. The intrepid explorer strode ahead with great determination and gusto, the cold wind blowing in his face. Behind him crept a crocodile of shivering children with Miss Pruitt, as usual, at the back, trying to keep up.

'Come on! Come on, you slow-coaches!' Mr Risley-Newsome barked impatiently, without looking back.

Nine

The 'Phantom Horseman'

'I don't reckon anything to this,' gasped Michael Chan to Dominic. 'Walking for miles and miles in freezing winds, through mud and water, soaked to the skin. It's supposed to be a school trip to look at the countryside and the coast, not an army survival exercise.'

'Is that your voice I can hear, Dominic Dowson?' boomed Mr Risley-Newsome from in front. 'If it is, save your breath for the walk ahead. We've a long way to go and I've heard quite enough from you today.'

Firstly, Dominic thought, *I have not said a word since we started and secondly, why did 'Old Grisly-Gruesome' always assume it was him? Well*, he said to himself, *just so long as he doesn't discover I'm not wearing boots, I shall be happy enough*.

He wished for the umpteenth time that he had brought his boots. His feet were cold and wet and caked in mud already and the party had barely set off, and he kept slipping and sliding on the wet grass and muddy paths. The trainers had started life a bright blue and white but now were a dirty brown colour. *Still*, thought Dominic, *they are much less easy to spot in this state*.

When the children finally reached the old railway bridge they were panting like exhausted greyhounds, their breath forming great clouds in the cold winter air.

'We'll stop here for five minutes,' said Mr Risley-Newsome, 'to recharge our batteries before the climb.'

'Climb!' exclaimed Michael, out of the teacher's earshot. 'We're off up a mountain now! A day in the country. It's like a trip up the Himalayas – wet and windy, cold and misty.'

'I'm just about ready to drop,' moaned Gerald.

'Excuse me! Did you say something, Dowson?' snapped Mr Risley-Newsome, swivelling round and stabbing a gloved finger in the direction of Dominic.

'Gerald was just saying, sir, that he was ready for a stop,' replied Dominic.

'Yes, well don't start getting comfortable, we're only staying here a short time. Now, gather round everybody, I've got something to say.' This was the introduction to yet another lecture. 'For the last half a

96

mile, as you all probably have noticed, we have been walking in a sort of valley. Now, it is not a natural valley cut into the rock by the ice, millions of years ago, like the ones I told my pupils about in geography last term. This sort of valley – are you listening to me, you boys at the back?'

'Yes, sir,' chorused Michael, Sean and Dominic.

'I hope you are.'

'We are, sir.'

'Good. As I was saying, this is not a natural valley, but one that has been man-made. It has been carved out of the landscape for the railway that went from Whitby to Scarborough. Trees, bushes and heather were bound in sheepskins and used to create a firm base in boggy areas. We've been walking along the old railway line which would, of course, have been a very stupid and dangerous thing to do had we been doing so a hundred years ago –'

'Sir, that would have been difficult,' said Nathan. 'It would mean I'd be one hundred and eleven years old, sir, and you would be –'

'Excuse me! I do not recall asking for comments.'

'Perhaps I might say a word,' said Miss Pruitt, moving to the front.

'Yes, of course,' said Mr Risley-Newsome, rather taken aback.

'A hundred years ago, children,' said Miss Pruitt, enthusiastically, 'this would have been a very busy railway line. Steam trains would have been speeding along through the English countryside, billowing clouds of smoke and bursting out of the tunnel mouth ahead of us. Just think of it. Children would be waving from the bridge. You'd have heard the screeching whistle and the sound of the wheels going *clickety clack, clickety clack* on the track.'

'Like the sound of my chattering teeth,' whispered Sean.

'There would have been elegant ladies and gentlemen,' continued the teacher, 'smartly dressed stewards, waiters and guards in their uniforms. When the big steam engine and the glistening carriages pulled into Scarborough, the station master would be on the platform, checking the arrival on his great gold pocket watch. He'd be dressed in a silk hat, black morning coat with a carnation in the button-hole, the ends of his moustache waxed to points, and he would walk up and down the brightly-painted station –'

'Not like the stations today,' snorted Mr Risley-Newsome. 'Noisy, smelly, crowded places covered in litter and the trains are never on time.'

'And in those days,' continued Miss Pruitt, 'the trains had wonderful names: "Prince of Wales", "Lord St Vincent", "Coronation Scot", "Mallard". What a marvellous sight they must have been.'

Mr Risley-Newsome suppressed a yawn and glanced at his watch ostentatiously. 'Well,' he said, 'shall we continue, Miss Pruitt. We do have another mile to walk along the old track, then a brisk climb. We are rather behind schedule. We should have been here at Brandon Bridge fifteen minutes ago.

The sooner we make a move, the better.'

'Sir,' said Velma.

'Yes, what is it?' asked Mr Risley-Newsome.

'Is this Brandon Bridge?'

'Yes, it is. At least somebody in this party is listening to what I say.'

'Are we walking through the tunnel, sir, under the bridge?'

'Yes, we are,' said Mr Risley-Newsome.

'Under Brandon Bridge,' she said nervously.

'Yes, *under* Brandon Bridge,' repeated the teacher impatiently.

Dominic, Gerald, Sean and Michael all looked at each other. They did not need to say anything.

'There's nothing in there now,' Miss Pruitt reassured Velma, putting her arm round the girl's shoulder. 'All the trains have gone long ago.'

'It is rather dark in the tunnel,' explained Mr Risley-Newsome, peering ahead of him, 'but I have an extremely powerful torch which I use when I'm pot-holing, and if everybody stays together and behaves themselves, we'll soon be through it. Now, it might be rather muddy underfoot in the tunnel, so keep to the sides and stay together.'

'But, sir,' persisted Velma, 'this is Brandon Bridge.'

'Yes, I have just told you it is Brandon Bridge. Is there something wrong with your hearing?'

'What about the ghost?' asked Velma.

'Ghost!' snorted Mr Risley-Newsome. 'What ghost?'

'Sir, there's a ghost in the tunnel!'

'Don't be so ridiculous!' snapped the teacher. 'Whoever's told you such nonsense?'

'But, sir, there *is* a ghost. Miss Brewster told us about it last night when we were helping to wash the dishes. She said there's a ghost in the tunnel.'

'Stuff and nonsense!' snapped Mr Risley-Newsome.

'Sir,' said Nathan Thomas in a rather uncertain tone of voice, 'do we have to go through the tunnel? It does look really dark and spooky.'

'It does look dark,' said Darren, peering ahead of him, 'and spooky.'

'Of course it looks dark, you silly boy. There's no light inside a tunnel. Now, let us press on. There's nothing whatsoever to be afraid of.' Mr Risley-Newsome looked at Velma. 'And you, young lady, will you stop putting silly ideas about ghosts and the like into people's heads.'

'But, sir, Miss Brewster says it's been seen by lots and lots of people. Sir, Miss Brewster says –'

'Excuse me!' snapped the teacher. 'I'm not the slightest bit interested in what Miss Brewster, or anyone else for that matter, has to say. Filling your heads with such nonsense. I'm telling you, there are no such things as ghosts and there is nothing in that tunnel but a rather muddy bit of ground.'

'Come along, children,' urged Miss Pruitt. Then she added mischievously, 'Mr Risley-Newsome will be ahead of us all the time and if there is a ghost I am sure he will be able to deal with it.' *Like everything else*, she thought to herself.

Mr Risley-Newsome, with a less determined step, led the way to the entrance of the tunnel. He paused and shone his torch into the darkness. It certainly did look rather sinister, like some great yawning black mouth, and smelt rather unpleasant.

'I'm not going in there,' said Gerald determinedly. 'I'm not going in there whatever he says.'

'And I'm not,' said Sean firmly.

'Nor me,' added Michael.

'It's only a story,' said Dominic, trying to convince himself. 'There aren't such things as ghosts.'

Mr Risley-Newsome swivelled round. 'Stop all this idle chatter, you children, and follow me.'

'But, sir, it might be in the tunnel,' cried Nathan Thomas.

'Yeah, it might be in the tunnel,' echoed Darren.

'What might be in the tunnel?' asked Mr Risley-Newsome.

'Whatever it is that's in the tunnel, sir,' replied Darren.

Miss Pruitt stepped forward. 'What exactly did Miss Brewster say was in the tunnel, Velma?'

'Miss, it's the "Phantom Horseman", miss,' explained Velma. 'It was over a hundred years ago, when the trains were running along this line, that the hunt chased a fox down this embankment. The hounds nearly caught it, but it ran into the tunnel to escape. The first huntsman in a red coat and black hat went in after the fox, miss. He rode into the tunnel.'

'And?' asked Miss Pruitt.

'A train was coming from the other end, miss. The huntsman was never seen alive again, but his ghost gallops up and down the track, looking for the fox. Miss Brewster told us that sometimes the engine drivers see the "Phantom Horseman" in his red coat galloping after a ghostly fox. Hikers and ramblers have also seen him on the embankment, staring down with great luminous eyes and breathing smoke.'

'I'm not going through that tunnel, miss,' said Nathan.

'Neither am I,' said Darren.

'Neither am I,' said several other children.

'We are *all* going through that tunnel,' said Mr Risley-Newsome angrily, 'and we are going through it this minute. I do not want to hear any more about the phantom huntsman with the luminous eyes. Right, stay close to me.' With that he strode on ahead. He turned to see a group of static children watching him. 'Well, come on, look sharpish!'

Mr Risley-Newsome led the way, followed by a nervous group of children who clustered round Miss Pruitt like chicks round a mother hen. The entrance to the tunnel was dark and musty, the walls black with grime and the domed roof white and eerie-looking. All was blackness, save for the wide beam of the teacher's torch which formed a long golden passage of light ahead of them.

'It's like a tomb,' whispered Dominic to Sean.

'Like the tunnel of doom,' whispered Michael.

'Like a dark, spooky cellar,' whispered Velma.

'It's like creeping into a crypt,' whispered Gerald.

'I don't like this,' whispered Nathan, who was at the back.

'I don't like it, either,' whispered Darren.

'Stop that whispering!' hissed Mr Risley-Newsome. He sounded less confident now.

'Sir!' shouted Dominic. 'There's something there!'

'Where?' everyone chorused.

Mr Risley-Newsome suddenly stopped dead in his tracks. His torch picked out two luminous eyes ahead, glaring at him in the darkness. They were great, round, shining eyes staring from the end of the dark tunnel. A heavy, distant breathing like a winter wind could be heard, and in the light of the torch great clouds of white smoke billowed. The teachers and their pupils froze.

'It's th-th-th-th-the "Ph-Ph-Ph-Ph-Ph-Phantom H-H-H-H-Horseman",' stuttered Nathan.

'Th-th-th-th-th– "Ph-Ph-Ph-Ph– H-H-H-H-H-Horseman",' spluttered Darren.

Their voices echoed down the tunnel.

'He's coming . . .' wailed Nathan.

'To get us,' wailed Darren.

Dominic peered into the darkness. There was certainly something there, breathing heavily and staring at them with shining eyes. He felt his heart thumping in his chest. His throat went dry and his breath came in short bursts. *I don't believe in ghosts*, he told himself. *I don't believe in ghosts.*

'It's the "Phantom Horseman",' wailed Gerald.

'He's coming for us,' moaned Velma.

Mr Risley-Newsome turned to face the children. He saw a mass of shining eyes in the darkness and heard their frightened breathing. 'I want you all to go back out of the tunnel, slowly and sensibly.' There was a slight tremble in his voice. 'No running. No silliness. Just walk slowly back the way we came. Could you lead on, Miss Pruitt?' He shone the torch ahead of them and saw the children creeping back to the entrance. Behind him he heard the breathing getting closer and closer, and heard the heavy thud of hoofs on the earth echoing through the tunnel. As if walking through a minefield, Mr Risley-Newsome tiptoed after the children.

A minute later he and the children were out in the winter sunlight. Then everyone, in the cold light of day, was chattering and shouting, laughing and jumping.

'Miss, I saw it!' shouted Nathan.

'I saw it too,' echoed Darren.

'It had big shining eyes like lamps,' said Michael.

'Its face was as white as snow!' shouted Sean.

'And it was breathing smoke like a dragon,' added Dominic, still trembling a little but feeling massively relieved. In the bright light of day, the ghost or whatever it was did not seem very frightening. Ghosts are the creatures of the night, of graveyards and spooky castles.

'It was really, really horrible,' shivered Nathan, rubbing his hands together.

'Horrible,' said Darren. 'Really, really horrible.'

'Move away up the embankment, all of you,' ordered Mr Risley-Newsome, whose face was the colour of the grey stones of the bridge. 'Move right away from the track.'

Dominic watched the children clambering excitedly up the bank as Mr Risley-Newsome walked charily to the entrance and peered into the tunnel. They had certainly seen something in there, something with great, glassy, round eyes, a creature which puffed clouds of steam and pounded the earth with heavy hoofs. Suddenly there was a galloping sound. Dominic had never seen anybody move quite as quickly as Mr Risley-Newsome that morning. He shot down the track as fast as a rabbit with its tail on fire.

'Back! Get back!' he shouted as he scrambled up the embankment, dropping his torch and losing his woolly hat in the process.

Something emerged from the tunnel.

'Look! Look!' shouted Dominic from the bank.

The children stared at the entrance to the tunnel as the creature came out into the light. It was a big black-and-white cow which stopped suddenly, stared around with gentle brown eyes and breathed clouds of steamy breath in the cold air. Everyone cheered and a broad smile crossed the lips of Miss Pruitt.

'There's your "Phantom Horseman"!' she laughed. 'A cow, just an ordinary cow, sheltering in the tunnel for warmth. I'll give you "Phantom Horseman", Velma.'

Mr Risley-Newsome did not find it in the least bit amusing and scowled angrily.

As the animal ambled away in search of grass, another creature crept from the tunnel: a fox, the colour of the russet-red bracken that lined the old track. It stopped when it caught sight of Dominic staring down, then stood proudly for a moment, framed by the arc of the tunnel entrance. Before the creature scampered up the bank and disappeared into the brambles and bushes, Dominic could have sworn he saw a suggestion of a smile on its face.

'Did you see that?' Dominic asked Gerald.

'What?'

'The fox.'

Gerald sighed. 'You and your stories,' he said.

'There was a fox, there really was. It came out of the tunnel.'

'You're a great storyteller, Dominic,' said his friend.

'Come along, children.' It was Miss Pruitt's cheerful voice. 'Let's get moving. On to the track and wait for Mr Risley-Newsome to lead us through the tunnel.'

'I think, after all, Miss Pruitt, we will go back by the old footpath instead,' announced Mr Risley-Newsome, obviously still quite shaken.

It is interesting, Dominic thought to himself as he sat on the bank, *that 'Old Grisly-Gruesome' is not quite the expert he imagines himself to be and he does not seem quite as bursting with confidence as he did at the start of the walk.*

Ten

Grounded!

Next morning there was a real buzz in the air. The topic of conversation at breakfast was, of course, the 'Phantom Horseman'.

'I don't think I've ever been as frightened,' Gerald told Dominic and his friends. 'What with that spooky story the night before and then when we actually went into the tunnel, I could hear my heart beating, I was so scared.'

'Do you reckon there really is a "Phantom Horseman"?' asked Michael.

'Well, I wouldn't go through that tunnel,' said Sean. 'No way! I've never seen a ghost, but my Auntie Kath who lives in Ireland, she's heard one. It's called a banshee and when somebody's going to die it moans and groans and howls.'

'Could have just been the wind,' said Gerald. 'Anyway, can we change the subject? When I heard the hoofs and saw the smoky breath and those great luminous eyes, my heart was in my boots.'

'And speaking of boots,' said Michael, 'I think you've got away with it, Dom. "Old Grisly-Gruesome" never noticed your trainers.'

'He was too scared of the "Phantom Horseman",' said Dominic. 'Did you see his face when he came out of the tunnel? I wish I'd had a camera.'

'And when he was clomping down the track,' added Sean, 'in those great big boots . . .'

'Dropping his extremely powerful torch which he uses when he's potholing . . .' said Michael.

'And that daft woolly hat,' laughed Gerald.

'What are you laughing at, "Ginger-Nut"?' asked Nathan Thomas, who was listening in to the conversation.

'I don't like to be called "Ginger-Nut",' replied Gerald.

'Oooo, he doesn't like to be called "Ginger-Nut",' said Nathan in a silly voice.

'Well, we're calling you "Ginger-Nut", aren't we, Nath?' said Darren.

'Yeah, we are.'

'So, what are you laughing at, "Ginger-Nut"?' asked Nathan again.

'You've changed your tune this morning, Nathan,' said Dominic, coming to his friend's rescue. '"It's th-th-th-th-the 'Ph-Ph-Ph-Ph-Ph-Phantom H-H-H-H-Horseman'".'

'I wasn't scared,' said Nathan, blustering. 'I was just cold.'

'I wasn't scared, either,' echoed Darren.

'You didn't sound it,' said Dominic. 'You two nearly wet yourselves, you were so terrified.'

'No, we didn't!' cried Nathan.

'We weren't scared at all,' said Darren. 'Not of any old bull.'

'It was a cow,' sighed Nathan. 'It wasn't a bull, it was a cow.'

'Oh, yeah,' said Darren. 'Well, we weren't afraid of any old cow, either.'

Further discussion halted when Mr Risley-Newsome rose to speak. 'May I have your attention?' he said. He waited until the dining room was quiet and the pupils were looking his way. 'After the breakfast things have been cleared away, washed, dried and stacked, I want you all to assemble outside the youth hostel for today's walk. Make sure you are appropriately equipped with anorak, jumper, waterproofs, gloves, scarves and, of course, your clipboard, worksheets and sharp pencil. On today's excursion we will be walking along the clifftop from Whitby to Saltwick Bay. It's a more strenuous walk than yesterday's and quite a bit longer.' There was a great sigh from the children. 'Excuse me!' snapped the teacher. When silence returned, he continued. 'In Whitby we will see the Tuscan-style town hall which dates from the eighteenth century and some interesting shops along Church Street.'

'There's a very good bookshop on Church Street,' added Miss Pruitt. 'We may have time to have a browse and buy a book or postcard, so bring some money.'

'I don't think we have time to visit any shops, Miss Pruitt,' said Mr Risley-Newsome. 'Our schedule is very tight. We will, however, have the opportunity, provided a service is not taking place, to call in at the parish church of St Mary which has a magnificent tiered pulpit with ear trumpets and box pews and a fine Norman chancel arch. This is a much finer example of architecture than we saw in the church we visited on the first day. Nearby is the towering ruin of Whitby Abbey, built nearly nine hundred years ago, and famous for St Hilda. More about St Hilda later.'

Dominic noticed Miss Pruitt, sitting staring at the ceiling. She looked fed-up. *It must be truly dreadful for her*, Dominic thought, *to have to put up with 'Old Grisly-Gruesome', always taking charge, ordering her about and disagreeing with her all the time.* How lucky he was to have Miss Pruitt for a teacher and not him.

'The town is also famous for Captain James Cook,' continued Mr Risley-Newsome. 'Captain Cook was born near Whitby, in a village called Great Ayton –'

'Excuse me, sir,' said Gerald, waving his hand in the air.

'What is it, Fairclough?'

'It says in my pocket guide to Whitby that Captain Cook was born at Marton in Cleveland. It says he moved to Great Ayton as a boy, when his father became a bailiff there, and that's where he went to school.'

'Well, in my book he was born in Great Ayton,' said Mr Risley-Newsome. 'Now, Captain Cook was one of the greatest circumnavigators of the world –'

'And of course Whitby is famous for Dracula,' said Miss Pruitt, rising to her feet. Dominic could see that she had had enough of the lecture. 'The author who wrote the story of Dracula, Bram Stoker, mentions Whitby in his spine-chilling tale of the most famous of all vampires.' Dominic could see by everyone's faces and the way that they all sat up that there was a whole lot more interest now. 'In fact, every year there is a Dracula Festival.'

'Wow!' exclaimed Sean.

'And the town is full of people wearing black capes and vampire teeth.'

'Is it on now, miss?' asked Sean.

'No, I don't think so, but there is the "Dracula Experience", a sort of exhibition in the town.'

'Could we go, miss?' asked Velma.

'I don't know whether we have the time,' replied the teacher, giving Mr Risley-Newsome a sideways glance.

'I think we heard quite enough about spooks and spectres yesterday in the tunnel, Miss Pruitt,' said

Mr Risley-Newsome. 'I am sure the exhibition is most interesting, but it is not on my itinerary.' The children groaned.

What a stick in the mud he is, thought Dominic.

'Now, we should be making a start if we are to keep to the programme I have planned for the day. Before we set off, let me mention a few do's and don'ts. One: there are many potential dangers on clifftop walks – fierce winds, crumbling rocks, deep potholes and slippery footpaths –'

'And vampire bats,' said Sean under his breath.

'Excuse me? Did someone say something?' Mr Risley-Newsome scanned the faces before him. 'If someone has something to say, then let him share it with us all, rather than mumbling inaudibly under his breath. Was it you, Dowson?'

'No, sir,' replied Dominic, shuffling into a position where the teacher could not see his trainers.

'I hope not.'

'It wasn't. I never opened my mouth.'

'Don't take that tone with me, young man,' started the teacher.

'Mr Risley-Newsome,' said Miss Pruitt, coming to Dominic's rescue, 'as you said earlier, we should be making a start if we are going to keep to the itinerary which you have planned.'

'Yes, that's right,' Mr Risley-Newsome conceded, consulting his watch. 'So, everyone be at the front of the building in half an hour.'

When the pupils, with cold faces and glum expressions, had assembled outside the youth hostel, Mr Risley-Newsome gave a final warning. 'Now, remember what I said. This is a potentially hazardous walk, so I want everyone to be very vigilant.'

'Sir,' said Nathan, waving his hand in the air.

Here it comes, thought Dominic. He had seen Nathan Thomas looking at his trainers earlier and smirk before nudging Darren Wilmott and whispering something. He must have heard Michael mention the word 'boots' at breakfast. Now he was going to inform Mr Risley-Newsome. Dominic just knew it and then there would be fireworks.

'What is it, Thomas?'

'Sir, you know what you were saying about wearing the right clothes?'

'Yes.'

'And that everyone needs to have the appropriate gear.'

'What about it?'

'Well, sir, wouldn't it be better if Dominic wore boots instead of the trainers that he is wearing?'

Mr Risley-Newsome's eagle eyes glinted and then focused on Dominic's feet. When he caught sight of the trainers his mouth screwed up savagely.

'Do you ever listen, Dowson?' he demanded, spitting out the words. 'Do you take any notice what-soever of what people have to say? Too busy talking or daydreaming. I must have mentioned the need to wear appropriate clothing and proper footwear more times than you have had hot dinners. Get back into the youth hostel and put on your boots and be quick about it.'

'I can't, sir,' replied Dominic quietly, looking down at his feet.

'There is no such word as "can't" in my vocabulary, Dowson. Now, do as you are told and get your boots on and smartly. We haven't got all day.'

'Sir, I can't. I haven't got any boots,' said Dominic.

'No boots! No boots!' spluttered the teacher.

'Where are they, Dominic?' asked Miss Pruitt calmly.

'They're at home, miss. I forgot to bring them.'

'Oh, Dominic,' she sighed.

'Typical!' sneered Mr Risley-Newsome. 'The most important article of all and you forget to bring them.' He took a blustering breath. 'Well, one thing is certain and that is you are not coming on today's excursion. You will remain in the youth hostel.'

'I am sure that if Dominic kept well away from the cliff edge –' began Miss Pruitt.

Dominic knew she was fighting a losing battle. There was not a chance in the world of 'Old Grisly-Gruesome' allowing him to go.

Mr Risley-Newsome gave a little laugh. It was not a pleasant laugh. 'That is out of the question, Miss Pruitt. There is no possibility, no possibility at all, of my taking a pupil, particularly when that pupil happens to be a walking disaster like Dowson, on a potentially hazardous trip along the cliff path and across the beach. One thing I do pride myself on is

114

safety and I am not putting him, or indeed any pupil, at needless risk.' He swung round to glower at Dominic. 'You will remain in the youth hostel and complete an essay entitled: "Why it is important to wear the appropriate footwear when out walking".'

'Yes, sir,' replied Dominic. *This trip has been brilliant so far*, he thought – *one of the best times in my life.* He loved the sea and the long sandy beaches, the screech of the gulls and the fresh salty air. Now that had all come to an end. He would be made to stay for the rest of the week inside the youth hostel by himself, writing essays when he really wanted to be outside.

Miss Pruitt appealed to the pupils who stood watching proceedings with awed expressions. 'Has anyone, by any chance, a spare pair of boots which might fit Dominic?'

She was faced with blank expressions and a few shakes of the head.

'Miss Pruitt,' said Mr Risley-Newsome, 'we are already ten minutes behind schedule. According to my itinerary we should be on the coastal footpath by now.'

'Very well,' said Miss Pruitt, resigned to the situation. 'Dominic, you had better stay here today and we will discuss what to do when we return.'

'Yes, miss,' said Dominic. 'Sorry, miss.'

'These things happen, Dominic,' she said sympathetically. 'It's just that they seem to happen to you rather more than to anyone else.'

'And you won't be setting foot out of the youth

hostel until you have boots on your feet,' added Mr Risley-Newsome, determined to have the last word.

Dominic took off his rucksack and made his way sadly, head down, through the crowd of pupils.

'Hard luck, Dom,' said Michael, patting him on the back.

'Yeah, hard luck, Dom,' said Gerald.

'Somebody ought to push that Nathan Thomas off the cliff,' said Velma, giving the boy in question such an angry look.

Dominic was not really listening to his friends. He was too upset. He did, however, catch part of the conversation between his teacher and the informer.

'How very thoughtful of you, Nathan,' said Miss Pruitt, approaching Nathan Thomas. Her voice was full of sarcasm.

'Pardon, miss?' the boy replied, with the most innocent of expressions on his face.

'I said, how very thoughtful of you to point out Dominic's trainers to Mr Risley-Newsome.'

'Miss, I was just trying to be helpful. I mean, something might have happened to Dominic if he was not wearing boots.'

'Oh, yes, Nathan, I am sure you were trying to be helpful. You are *such* a helpful and considerate boy, aren't you?'

'But, miss –'

'Oh, do be quiet, Nathan Thomas,' said Miss Pruitt, quickly moving away.

Dominic watched sadly from the library window as

116

the teachers and pupils crunched off down the gravel drive. So that was it. There would be no long walks along the sandy beaches for him, no clifftop rambles or visits to Whitby, no hikes across the lonely moors or boat trips. The words of 'Old Grisly-Gruesome' went round and round in his head: 'And you won't be setting foot out of the youth hostel until you have boots on your feet.'

Eleven

Daisy Disappears

'And what are you doing here?' asked Miss Brewster when she found Dominic sitting in the library, staring thoughtfully out of the window. 'You should be out getting some fresh sea air in your lungs, not sitting inside. Are you not feeling well?'

'No, I'm fine Miss Brewster,' replied Dominic, and then he explained the problem.

'Boots!' she said. 'Is that all?'

'It's enough,' said Dominic sadly. 'Without boots I can't go on any of the trips. I shall have to stop here, in the youth hostel.'

'Well, we'll just have to find you some boots, then, won't we?'

'Easier said than done,' said Dominic morosely. 'Where would I get a pair of size six boots from? They don't just drop out of the sky.'

'You never know,' chuckled Miss Brewster. 'You never know.'

Later that morning Dominic, having finished the essay for Mr Risley-Newsome, was drawn to the kitchen by the delicious aroma of freshly-baked bread. He found Miss Brewster standing behind a large pine table in the middle of the great white-walled room, punching a huge mountain of dough with fat floury fists.

'I thought it wouldn't be too long before you found your way down here,' she said.

'I just wondered if you wanted any jobs doing,' said Dominic. 'I am the world's best potato-peeler, washer-upper, shoe-shiner, shelf-duster and carpet-cleaner.'

'And a pretty good bread-taster, I'll be bound,' said Miss Brewster, smiling.

'I certainly wouldn't say no to a slice,' said Dominic, eyeing a large, brown, crusty loaf, cooling on the table before him.

'Well, it's just come out of the oven,' said Miss Brewster. 'You can have a nice thick crust with your lunch. Oh, and there is a little job I would like you to do for me.'

'Yeah, of course,' said Dominic. 'What is it, Miss Brewster?'

'I've been so busy today, what with the baking and such, that I haven't had time to take Daisy out.' At the mention of her name the terrier pricked up her ears, jumped out of her basket and began running around in circles, wagging her fat stumpy tail. 'Just look at her. Would you take her for me?'

'I can't, Miss Brewster,' replied Dominic. 'I'm not allowed out of the youth hostel unless I have boots on.'

'I know that,' said Miss Brewster. 'Well, a funny thing happened after our little conversation in the library. I was going out to the dustbins and a pair of size six boots just dropped out of the sky.' Miss Brewster reached down and produced a pair of boots from underneath the table. They were an expensive-looking pair in light-brown leather with thick, blue, moulded-rubber soles and bright-yellow laces.

'Where are they from?' gasped Dominic.

'They just fell out of the sky.'

'No, really, Miss Brewster.'

'You're not the only person in the world, you know, who forgets things. I have lots of school parties here over the year and there's always somebody who forgets something when he goes back home. I've enough lost property to start an outdoor-clothing shop. I've got anoraks, scarves, gloves, rucksacks, socks, shirts, shorts, vests and underpants. I've also got a selection of boots, including a size six, perfect for a young man who just happens to have left his own at home. Come on, then, aren't you going to try them on?'

The boots fitted snugly and Dominic's face broke into a great beaming smile. 'They're perfect!'

'Now, you're all set to take Daisy for her run,' said Miss Brewster. 'Stay at the front of the house. There are the cliffs at the back and it's steep and slippery. She's a little devil for chasing rabbits near the cliff edge is Daisy, and given half a chance will be round the back. The way she runs after them, she'll fall over the clifftop one of these days.'

'I'll look after her, Miss Brewster,' said Dominic. 'She's as safe as houses with me.'

Dominic, wrapped up in his anorak, scarf and gloves and wearing his 'new' boots, set off down the wide gravel drive at the front of the youth hostel with a spring in his step and with Daisy scampering excitedly beside him. He turned to look back at the dark forbidding building. The windows stared down at him like cold eyes, the writhing ivy whispered in the wind and the branches in the tall sycamore tree creaked ominously. *I wouldn't like to be here by myself on a dark night*, Dominic said to himself. He shivered.

Daisy scurried off ahead of him and began snuffling and scratching happily in the overgrown borders surrounding the mossy lawn. After ten minutes of exploring, burrowing and sniffing, Daisy raced back to Dominic's side, panting madly.

'It's colder than I thought out here,' Dominic told the little terrier, patting her fat round body and shivering. His ears tingled, his cheeks stung and his nose began to run. 'I think we'll head back.' He thought of

121

the warm kitchen, a steaming cup of hot sweet tea and a thick wedge of freshly-made bread with butter and strawberry jam. It was just too appealing. And that's when Daisy saw the rabbit.

It was munching away merrily in a clump of spiky grass when the dog caught sight of it. The terrier made a low grumbling noise and then bounded off at high speed in the creature's direction. The startled rabbit shot round the side of the house with a flash of white tail and a yelping Daisy in hot pursuit.

'Daisy! Daisy!' shouted Dominic, running after her. 'Come back!'

To the rear of the house a dismal rain-soaked land-scape dropped away sharply to a low wire fence which skirted the cliff edge.

'Daisy! Daisy!' called Dominic frantically. 'Come here, girl! Daisy, where are you?'

Then he spotted her racing in the direction of the church after the terrified rabbit. The dog disap-peared over a grassy hillock. Dominic's heart began to pound in his chest and, despite the cold wind, his face was now hot with panic. With a sinking feeling in the pit of his stomach, he recalled Miss Brewster's warning not to go round the back of the house, near the steep cliff edge. He thought of Miss Pruitt's com-ment that trouble always seemed to follow him about and Mr Risley-Newsome's words about him being a nuisance of the first order, a number one mischief-maker, a storyteller, a 'ne'er-do-well'. He would be in real trouble yet again if Daisy disappeared. Dominic could picture what would happen if he returned to the youth hostel without the dog: Miss Brewster distraught and weeping, Miss Pruitt sighing and despairing and Mr Risley-Newsome fuming mad.

'Oh, Daisy,' he moaned, 'where have you gone?'

Just as a deep-seated dread was beginning to set in, he heard an excited yelping in the distance. Dominic set off running in the direction of the noise. He soon found himself in front of the square, squat, grey church with the red, rusting, iron railings.

'Daisy!' he shouted, looking all around him. 'Daisy, where are you?'

His cries were answered by a frantic barking, coming from the overgrown wooded area to the front of the church.

A few moments later Dominic found himself in a strange, dark, overgrown world of gnarled trees, choking briars and twisting thorns, moss-covered logs and creeping ivy. The copse smelt of rotting wood, mouldy mushrooms and wild garlic and felt very, very eerie and unwelcoming. Ignoring the prickles and the sharp branches which scratched at his face, Dominic pushed deeper into the tangled jungle in the direction of the yapping. The barking suddenly stopped. Save for the crunching of his feet on the fallen branches, all was silent.

'Daisy! Daisy!' shouted Dominic. 'Where are you?'

Again his heart missed a beat when there came an answering yelp. It sounded as if the dog's barking was coming from some long, echoey tunnel. Dominic tugged and pushed, pulled and trampled his way into a small clearing. The barking seemed to be coming from directly beneath him. He put his ear to the ground and heard the dog yapping and yelping for all she was worth. Next Dominic started scratching away the branches and leaves and tugging up tussocks of grass and weeds until his fingers felt something hard and metallic.

It was a large, rusting ring of iron set in a slab of pale-grey stone. To the side was a hole, just about big enough for a small dog to scramble through.

'Daisy!' Dominic shouted. 'Are you down there?' There was a whining response. 'How did you get down there, you silly dog?'

He thought for a moment or two how he might get her out. Then he cleared the rest of the weeds and branches to expose the square of stone. It looked like a sort of trapdoor. He tugged at the metal ring, but the slab would not budge.

'Don't worry, Daisy. I'll get you out!' he shouted down the hole.

Get her out, he thought, *but how? Think Dominic*, he said to himself. *Keep calm and use your brains. The dog's trapped down a hole but doesn't sound in any pain*. With a torch, a spade and length of rope, he reckoned he could rescue her if only he could move the stone slab.

Dominic hurried back to the youth hostel. Through his mind rushed the most amazing thoughts. Might he have discovered the smugglers' tunnel? There might be a secret passageway beneath the ground leading to a cave stacked with treasure. He might be the first person to go in there in two hundred years.

Having collected his torch from the bedroom, a thick nylon rope from the tack room and a rusty spade which he found round the back of the house, Dominic hurried back to his discovery.

In no time at all he was in the clearing again, shouting into the darkness below him. 'I'm here, Daisy. I'll soon have you out.'

There was a whimpering from underground. Dominic hacked and dug at the earth round the slab and, using the spade as a lever, managed to move the stone inch by inch. He shone his torch into the blackness beneath it and gasped. The beam lit up a narrow flight of roughly hewn steps. Looking up were Daisy's shining eyes.

'It *is* a secret passage,' Dominic gulped. 'It's the one used by the smugglers. I just know it. No wonder the customs men couldn't find any trace of them. This tunnel must come from the beach, right up to the clifftop. Then they would have hidden their loot in the church.'

Dominic sat back on a mossy mound, ignoring Daisy's frantic barking. He imagined the smugglers, shrouded in long black cloaks, their hair stiff with salt, rowing ashore, unloading their illegal cargo on to the sandy beach, rolling the fat casks and heaving the heavy boxes across the rocks by the light of a pale moon. He could hear the swishing of the sea sweeping up the beach, the soft splash of the muffled oars in the water, the crunch of boots on the pebbles, the frantic shouts of the customs men on the clifftop and the crack of muskets. He was brought out of his reverie by the yelping from below.

'All right, Daisy, I'm coming, I'm coming!' he shouted down the hole.

Fixing the rope securely to the thick stump of a dead tree, Dominic lowered himself carefully into the blackness. The new boots, with their thick, rubber-moulded soles, were perfect for clambering down the slimy steps. One, two, three, four, five, six, he climbed before he felt Daisy jumping up excitedly.

'Down girl!' commanded Dominic. 'You'll make me lose my footing.'

He shone the torch and discovered he was standing on a large ledge, from which a further flight of narrow steps, chiselled into the rock, disappeared downwards. Daisy was now leaping up and barking furiously.

'All right, Daisy, all right!'

Dominic took a great breath, more out of relief than anything. The air below ground was icy cold and had an overpowering smell of seaweed and salt. Beneath him he could hear the distant slap, slap, slap of water on rock.

I knew I was right, he said to himself, rubbing his hands together to warm them. *This passage must lead right down to the beach. It is the smugglers' secret tunnel.*

Dominic directed the torch's beam around him. As his eyes became accustomed to the shadowy subterranean world, he could make out slimy walls, gaping caverns and a series of rusty iron rings set in the rock face at regular intervals, some with the remnants of rope hanging loosely from them.

'I knew it!' he said out loud. 'This *is* the smugglers' secret tunnel.' He picked up the frisky little creature which was leaping about his legs. 'I'm going on down,' Dominic told the dog, 'but you can't come with me, Daisy. It's too dangerous for you. I'm taking you back to the house.' He stroked the fat round head. 'And don't you go spilling the beans to Miss Brewster.'

Twelve

The Secret of Thundercliff Bay

Dominic ran to the youth hostel, the dog tucked underneath his arm and with his heart thumping away in his chest, but this time with excitement rather than panic. His head was full of wild, fantastic thoughts. Suppose there was treasure down there – chests of sparkling Spanish doubloons, caskets crammed with sapphires and rubies, diamond rings, pearl necklaces, emerald brooches, carved ivory figures, swords inlaid with gold and jewels, huge ivory tusks and boxes of rare objects.

He could just picture the scene when he returned home. He would wander into the living room. Mum would ask if he had had a nice time. 'Oh yes,' he would say casually. Gran would ask him what he had tucked underneath his arm. He would then flick open the treasure chest and let the coins fall to the floor like a waterfall of gold. 'I've brought you back a little present,' he would say.

He tried to control his excitement when he entered the kitchen.

'Just in time for lunch,' said Miss Brewster. 'Did you enjoy yourself?'

Amazing, phenomenal, extraordinary, incredible, astounding, unbelievable, Dominic thought to himself, but he answered vaguely, 'Oh yes, very nice.'

Daisy panted at his feet, looking up expectantly with her bright black eyes.

'You've certainly made friends with Daisy,' said Miss Brewster. 'She doesn't usually take to people like that. You've made quite an impression, Dominic. Was she good?'

'Perfect,' Dominic replied, patting the panting little dog, which was jumping up.

'She didn't go near those cliffs, did she?'

'Oh, no, Miss Brewster, not near the cliffs.'

'Well, that's good. Now, what about some lunch?'

'Could I have it later?' asked Dominic, eager to return to the secret passage. 'I thought I might have another little walk, this time without Daisy. Get used to the new boots.'

'Another walk? You're a glutton for punishment. Go on, then, I'll save you something for later.

But stay away from that cliff edge, won't you?'

Dominic ran back to the copse as quickly as his legs could carry him. Down the path, across the lawn, along the clifftop, until he came to the thicket. He fought his way through the bushes and brambles, crunching the twigs noisily underfoot until he came upon the slab of rock with the rusting iron ring and the tunnel. He hadn't dreamt it. It was real. The smugglers' secret tunnel.

Step by careful step he descended deep into the darkness, keeping the rope firmly grasped in one hand and the torch in the other. The beam of light illuminated a strange and damp world of dark caverns, gaping like the mouths of monsters, sculptured pillars, twisted fossilized formations, great rounded arches of stone, exotic carvings of jagged rock hanging like rotten teeth. The sound of the sea grew louder as he crept downwards. Soon it was no longer the rhythmic slap, slap, slap of water on rock he had heard earlier, but a thunderous crashing and smashing.

After what seemed to be many, many steps later, Dominic found himself in a spacious chamber with a moist sandy floor and a great domed roof. The sound of an angry sea filled the chamber. A shaft of light flooded upwards and shadows danced grotesquely on the slimy walls. Dominic shivered. Nervously, he edged towards the light and peered over a sharp overhanging ledge. Beneath him, a few metres down, was a small cave mouth into which the sea, in a frenzy of froth and foam, was hurling itself against the black seaweed-covered walls. This was the smugglers' cave for sure.

They would have unloaded their cargo, carried it into the cave, hoisted it up the rock face and then through the tunnel, and up the steps to the clifftop. But where was all the booty? Where were the chests of sparkling Spanish doubloons, caskets crammed with sapphires and rubies, diamond rings, pearl necklaces, emerald bracelets, swords inlaid with gold and jewels, boxes of rare objects? Where were the barrels of French brandy, the fat casks of dark Spanish wine, bales of tobacco and boxes of contraband? There was nothing but rock and water and sand.

Ah well, thought Dominic, *it's exciting all the same.* He had found the secret of the Thundercliff Bay smugglers and he might well become famous.

Dominic turned back, pulling himself up the steps slowly but surely with a great deal of heaving and grunting. He emerged into the light of day and took a deep breath of cold air. Sliding the slab of rock back in place, he left the rope where it was. He decided that he would come back and explore the secret passage again, as soon as he could.

At the youth hostel he returned the boots to the tack room, changed out of his wet clothes, had a shower and went in search of Miss Brewster.

Dominic was sitting in the kitchen, finishing a huge crust of freshly-baked bread, spread thickly with butter and jam, when he heard noises from the tack room.

'Sounds as if they're back,' remarked Miss Brewster. 'I didn't think they'd stay out much longer in this weather. It's turned bitter out there. You had best be going, Dominic. You don't want to get into any more trouble with Mr Double-Barrel, High-and-Mighty, do you?'

Stuffing the remaining bread and jam in his mouth, Dominic scurried off up the stairs.

Five minutes later, sour-faced Mr Risley-Newsome, as bad-tempered as ever, and a gloomy-looking Miss Pruitt, as usual following behind, found him poring over a book in the library with an expression of fierce concentration on his face.

'I trust you have completed the essay I set you, Dowson,' said Mr Risley-Newsome.

'Oh, yes, sir,' replied Dominic cheerfully, passing the teacher his exercise book.

'Well, I really don't know what we are going to do with you, Dominic,' sighed Miss Pruitt. 'Fancy forgetting your boots.'

'Typical,' mouthed her colleague. Mr Risley-Newsome flicked through the pages of the exercise book and arched an eyebrow. 'Well, it looks as if you will be writing a few more of these essays before we return to school, won't you?' He let the book drop on to the desk in front of him. 'Because, as I said before, there is not the slightest chance of you accompanying us on any trip without the appropriate footwear.'

'Yes, sir, I know that,' replied Dominic. He waited until the teacher had turned his back on him and started for the door before adding, 'I have some boots now, sir.'

Mr Risley-Newsome turned round sharply. 'You have some boots? From where, may I ask, have you suddenly acquired a pair of boots?'

'Miss Brewster found a spare pair in the tack room, sir. They had been left by someone from another school and they fit me like a glove.'

'Oh, that's excellent, Dominic,' cooed Miss Pruitt, obviously pleased.

'Fortunate for him, I should say.' Mr Risley-Newsome scrutinized Dominic's feet and grunted. 'And where are these boots?' he asked.

'In the tack room,' replied Dominic, glancing down at the teacher's mud-caked boots. 'You said we had to leave all our outdoor clothes and boots in the tack room, so we don't dirty the carpet.'

'So I did,' replied the teacher, departing. 'So I did.'

Miss Pruitt, suppressing a smile, picked up Dominic's exercise book and examined his essay. 'I have always thought that essays should be given to children as a treat and not as a punishment. Still, you seem to have made a very good effort here, Dominic. You weren't too bored by yourself all morning, were you?'

'Oh, no, miss.'

'Good.'

'How was the trip, miss?'

Miss Pruitt pulled a face. 'Cold, wet, windy and tiresome,' she replied. 'Still, there's only a couple of days to go.' The teacher gave a little smile. 'Dominic, is that jam round your mouth?'

After dinner Mr Risley-Newsome shuffled a thick wad of paper before him in preparation for another of his laborious lectures.

'Tomorrow we will be walking along part of the Cleveland Way. The name Cleveland comes from the old Norse word *Klifland* which, for your information, means "Land of cliffs".'

Now, there's a thing, thought Dominic, smiling. *Whoever would have thought that* Klifland *meant 'Land of cliffs'.*

'Is something amusing you, Dowson?' asked Mr Risley-Newsome, catching sight of the boy's grinning face.

'No, sir, I'm just feeling happy,' replied Dominic.

'Well, pay attention. The Cleveland Hills,' continued the teacher, 'form part of a range of unusually shaped scarps which are littered with Bronze Age tumuli and cairns. I shall be drawing your attention to these *en route* and we may have time to sketch them. In the seventeenth century alum was discovered . . .'

And so Mr Risley-Newsome's voice droned on. Dominic wasn't listening to a word. He was dreaming of the dark and dripping tunnel, the secret caves and caverns and the treasure that might be hidden there.

Later that evening, when the children were completing their lengthy worksheets about Whitby, St Mary's Church and Captain Cook, prepared in pleasure-destroying detail by Mr Risley-Newsome, Dominic headed for the library to get a book. He, of course, not having been on the trip, had escaped the exercise but had been told by Miss Pruitt to spend the time reading. When he heard the teachers' voices in the library, Dominic stood outside the half-open door to listen.

'May I know where we are going tomorrow?' Miss Pruitt was asking Mr Risley-Newsome.

'I thought I explained that after dinner, Miss Pruitt,' he replied in a mock-pleasant sort of voice. 'We will be walking along part of the Cleveland Way –'

'I mean, could I see the actual route itself?'

'Yes, of course,' he said.

Dominic peered round the door. Mr Risley-Newsome was pointing to a large Ordnance Survey map before him and tracing a line with his long finger.

'We are here, you see,' he said, tapping the map. 'We shall be following this designated footpath by Stainthorpe Farm, turning then on to this track here to get to the clifftop at Clayton Point. Following the route of the Cleveland Way, we shall find ourselves here, at Campbell's Point. The path drops down through woodland and, bearing right, we will reach the shore. Then after a mile or so's brisk walk across the sands at Thundercliff Wyke, we shall arrive at Capstan Cliffs and climb up this footpath to the clifftop just here and arrive back at the youth hostel.' He consulted his watch. 'I estimate it will take us about four hours at the most.'

Miss Pruitt examined the map for a moment and frowned.

'Is there something troubling you, Miss Pruitt?' asked her colleague.

'Isn't Thundercliff Wyke supposed to be quite hazardous?' she asked, examining the map.

'Is that a question, Miss Pruitt,' said Mr Risley-Newsome, 'or an observation?'

'I believe that Thundercliff Wyke is a dangerous stretch of coast.'

Mr Risley-Newsome sighed noisily. Dominic could see that he was none too pleased, but that he managed to keep a small, forced smile on his face. 'I am not aware that Thundercliff Wyke has a reputation for being dangerous,' he said. His good humour had disappeared like smoke in the wind.

'Miss Brewster,' Miss Pruitt continued, undeterred by his irritation, 'did mention to me that Thundercliff Wyke was rather rocky and secluded and that there are fast-rising tides.'

Mr Risley-Newsome made a little chuckling noise. 'Miss Pruitt,' he said, 'the whole of this coast is rather rocky and full of secluded bays with fast-rising tides.'

'I appreciate that –' she began.

'Every stretch of coast is potentially dangerous.'

'But I was told this particular stretch is notorious.'

Mr Risley-Newsome leaned back in his chair and breathed out heavily. 'Are you suggesting that we abandon tomorrow's trip, Miss Pruitt?' he asked. Before she could reply, he continued, 'A trip, I might add, which I have planned down to the very last detail?'

'I am merely mentioning that the area has a reputation for being dangerous. After all, Miss Brewster does live here and is familiar with the coast. Shall I ask her to have a word with you?'

'That is really not at all necessary,' replied Mr Risley-Newsome loftily. 'I do know what I am doing, Miss Pruitt, despite your obvious reservations. Trust me.'

'Could we perhaps miss that part of the walk?' she asked.

'No, we can't,' replied Mr Risley-Newsome sharply. 'To abandon our walk along the beach would mean me having to re-plan the whole excursion. I can assure you, Miss Pruitt, your concerns about Thundercliff Wyke are quite groundless.'

'Very well, Mr Risley-Newsome. I just hope we don't live to regret it.'

Dominic crept away. He thought to himself, *I just hope I find some time to return to the tunnel.*

Thirteen

Nathan Comes a Cropper

The next morning was bright and fresh when the teachers and children set off for Thundercliff Wyke. Mr Risley-Newsome strode out ahead at a brisk pace, attired in his dark-green anorak, corduroy trousers and large boots, with an assortment of appendages – whistle, compass, binoculars and map case – dangling as usual from his neck, and a rucksack strapped to his back. Miss Pruitt, in her bright-pink anorak, yellow slacks and orange boots, brought up the rear. Dominic, in his new boots, strode out with a confident step with Nathan and Darren sniggering behind him.

'Where did you get your boots from then, Dowson?' asked Nathan Thomas.

'Yeah, where are the boots from?' parroted Darren.

'Ignore him,' said Velma to Dominic.

'They're girls' boots,' said Nathan. 'Dowson's wearing girls' boots.'

'Girls' boots,' chortled Darren.

'I wouldn't be seen dead in those,' said Nathan.

'No, neither I would I,' said Darren.

Nathan started to chant, 'He's got girls' boots. He's got girls' boots.'

'Whoever's making that silly noise,' came a thundering voice from the front, 'be quiet!'

Dominic did ignore Nathan. He had too many things on his mind to bother with such stupid comments. 'I've found something,' he said to Velma under his breath.

'What?' she whispered.

'I've found a tunnel.'

'A tunnel!' she exclaimed.

'Sssh,' said Dominic, putting a finger to his lips. 'Keep your voice down.'

'Where?' asked Velma. 'In the house?'

'No, near the old church. At the front, in that overgrown copse. It's a secret tunnel leading from the cliffs to the beach. I found it yesterday when you were out walking. It's all dark and spooky and there are these slippery steps going all the way into the cliff. It's what the smugglers used to get their booty up from the beach.'

'Wow!' exclaimed Velma, her mouth dropping open.

Nathan, having failed to provoke a response from Dominic, soon became bored and turned his unwelcome attentions to another unfortunate pupil.

Dominic related the whole story to Velma. He had intended to keep his discovery to himself because he wanted to return to the tunnel alone. So far he'd managed to fight the temptation to spill the beans even to Smurph and Michael, but now he was just bursting to tell someone. And he had come to like and trust Velma. Anyway, she might be quite useful when it came to it. So he told her about Daisy getting lost, the dark jungle of weeds, bushes and dead trees, the slab of rock with the iron ring and the flight of slippery steps leading to the beach.

'Did you find anything else?' asked Velma, her eyes as wide and as round as saucers.

'You mean treasure? Naw, nothing like that, but there might be some hidden away down there and, if I get the chance, I'm going back to have another look. You can come if you like.'

'I wouldn't dare. I couldn't go down a dark tunnel.'

'Well, I'm going back. I just have to,' Dominic told her.

'But we're off home tomorrow,' said Velma. 'There won't be time.'

'I'll have to find the time,' said Dominic. 'It's too good a chance to miss. We could go tonight when everyone's in bed. Michael, Smurph and Gerald could come as well.'

'You're really brave, Dominic,' said Velma. 'I'd be too scared.'

The line of pupils suddenly came to a halt.

'We are now at Stainthorpe Farm!' Mr Risley-Newsome announced loudly from the front. 'Gather round, everyone.' When the teacher was surrounded by the children, he started another of his monologues. 'In a moment we will be approaching the clifftop. I do not need to remind you how dangerous it can be.' He glanced in the direction of Miss Pruitt, as if making a point. 'Stay well away from the edge and on the designated footpath at all times, no running, dawdling or silly behaviour.'

'And keep your eyes open, children,' said Miss Pruitt, 'and you may see the birds which live and feed on the seashore. Some of them nest and roost in the sheltered cracks and among the rocks. There's the cormorant with its long, hooked beak, the guillemot which lives in a colony, and the great black-backed gull, a large and very strong-winged bird which robs nests.'

'Yes, indeed,' said Mr Risley-Newsome. 'Now, we will soon be on part of the Cleveland Way, which stretches for over a hundred miles along the coast. We will have extensive views of Robin Hoods Bay, which is very similar to Thundercliff Bay, with its warren of steep streets and passageways, except it is rather more popular with visitors. And before anyone asks again, Robin Hoods Bay had nothing whatsoever to do with the outlaw who supposedly lived in Sherwood Forest.'

'Some people believe that Robin Hood did in fact stay here when he was evading capture by the Sheriff of Nottingham,' said Miss Pruitt.

'Another fanciful tale!' Mr Risley-Newsome told her. 'I have looked into this and it is a myth invented by someone with an overactive imagination – something to attract tourists no doubt. No, there is no truth in the story. It's rather like the far-fetched tale told by the vicar about smugglers and secret tunnels.'

If only he knew, thought Dominic smiling. *If only he knew* . . .

The children, cold and weary, eventually arrived at Thundercliff Wyke. They were glad of the rest, even if it did mean listening to another lecture from 'Old Grisly-Gruesome'.

'Now, if everyone is looking this way,' the teacher began. 'On your right you will see the cliffs. Have a look.' Bored faces looked to the right. 'On your left you will see the sea. Have a look.' Bored faces looked to the left. 'I do not want anyone up the cliffs or in the sea. Is that clear?'

'Yes, sir,' chorused the children.

'Also, this coast is full of caves and slippery rocks. On your right you will see the caves. Have a look.' Bored faces looked to the right.

Dominic surveyed the caves with a good deal of interest.

'Ahead, you will see the rocks. Have a look.' Bored faces looked ahead. 'I do not want anyone in the caves or on the rocks. Is that clear?'

'Yes, sir,' chorused the children.

Dominic was still staring intently at the caves.

'Is that clear, Dowson?'

'Yes, sir.'

'There is also a great deal of boulder clay on the beach. This is the brown, muddy mounds near the cliff bottom. It has slid down in the heavy rains and is also extremely dangerous. I do not want anyone stuck in the mud, so stay well away from that as well. Walk on the sands, stay off the rocks, keep away from the sea, do not go near the boulder clay and behave yourselves. Is that perfectly clear?'

'Yes, sir,' chorused the children.

'Many of you will, no doubt, be wondering what a "wyke" actually is,' said Mr Risley-Newsome. Actually, it had not crossed anyone's mind. '"Wyke" is a Viking word which means a narrow inlet, sheltered by headlands. The huge slabs of rock, which we shall be passing on our walk, show fine examples of ripple marks. These rocks were formed over one hundred and fifty million years ago.'

Fancy that, thought Dominic. He wished he was exploring the tunnel rather than listening to this dreary commentary.

'These slabs are the remains of a massive river delta which then covered this part of Yorkshire,' continued Mr Risley-Newsome.

'And keep your eyes open, children,' said Miss Pruitt, intent on getting her two-pennyworth in, 'and you may see some of the more interesting marine creatures which live and feed on the seashore. There are starfish, for example. They sit in the mud, sand and rocky pools and eat mussels, which they pull open with their tube feet. There are, of course, many crabs under the stones and the seaweed. If you come across a crab, look at the end of its shell. It's called a "pie-crust". There are also colourful sea anemones, but don't touch these because they have stinging tentacles. You may see some small fish in the rock pools. If you come across any interesting shells or fossils, pebbles or bits of jet, pop them in your rucksack and we will look at them when we are back at the youth hostel.'

'Yes, indeed,' said Mr Risley-Newsome. 'But I do not want any of you collecting half the beach or picking up fish heads, dead crabs or slimy seaweed. One or two shells, fossils or pebbles is quite sufficient, and don't dawdle. Now, we have a two-mile walk ahead of us and then a steep climb at the end, so we had better be moving.' There were sighs and moans from the children. 'Excuse me!' snapped the teacher. 'I do not recall asking for any opinions. We will be walking along the beach, then up the footpath to the clifftop and back to the youth hostel, so let's be making tracks.'

The hike across the beach was much harder than imagined. The fine, wet sand gave easily under the children's feet and made it difficult for them to walk at any speed. They had to negotiate the outcrops of black rocks, draped in dark and slippery seaweed, the rock pools and the long rivulets of muddy water which trickled from the cliffs across the sand and into the sea. And then it began to spit with rain.

They were about halfway across the beach when it happened. There was a high-pitched scream which echoed off the black cliffs. It sounded like a wounded animal caught in a snare.

Mr Risley-Newsome, at the head of the line of pupils, jumped as if he had been poked with a cattle prod. Dominic saw him swivel round and then he caught sight of Nathan Thomas sitting, screaming, on a carpet of seaweed, cradling his foot and squirming in agony. Mr Risley-Newsome rushed back towards him. Miss Pruitt, who was as usual bringing up the rear, rushed forwards. They arrived at the same time and were soon joined by Dominic and the rest of the pupils, who gathered round with inquisitive faces.

'Ooooooh! Ooooooh! Aaaaaaah! Aaaaaaah!' moaned Nathan. 'My foot! My foot!'

'Whatever have you done?' asked Miss Pruitt, bending over the writhing boy.

His moans turned into a direful howl.

'Do stop that dreadful caterwauling at once!' ordered Mr Risley-Newsome, reaching down to inspect the injured foot.

'Ooooooh! Ooooooh! Aaaaaaah! Aaaaaaah!' Nathan continued. 'My foot! My foot!'

'How did you manage to do that?' demanded Mr Risley-Newsome angrily.

'I-I-I . . . s-s-s-slipped on the r-r-r-r-rock, s-s-s-sir,' stuttered the boy, 'and my f-f-f-f-foot w-w-w-w-went down a c-c-c-crack!'

'Sir, he might have broken his ankle,' volunteered Sean.

'Excuse me?'

'He might have broken his ankle,' repeated the boy.

'Did I ask for an opinion?' enquired the teacher testily.

'No, sir,' replied the boy.

'Well, kindly keep your clever comments to yourself.' He turned back to the wriggling pupil on the seaweed.

Miss Pruitt gently moved Nathan's foot backwards and forwards.

He winced and sniffed and bit his bottom lip. 'Ooooooh! Ooooooh! It hurts, Miss. It really, really hurts.'

'Well, I don't think it's broken,' she told Mr Risley-Newsome. 'Just a bad sprain, I think.'

'Ooooooh! Ooooooh! Aaaaaaah! Aaaaaaah!' moaned Nathan.

'Will you desist from making that noise?' snapped Mr Risley-Newsome. 'It will not help matters, you screeching like a strangled cat.'

'Mr Risley-Newsome,' said Miss Pruitt quietly, 'might I deal with this? The boy is clearly very distressed and in some pain. Now, Nathan, do you think you can walk?'

'N-n-n-n-no, miss,' he blurted out, wiping his nose on the sleeve of his anorak. 'It really, really hurts.'

'You won't know whether you can walk or not,' observed Mr Risley-Newsome, 'until you try. Get up and put some weight on your foot.'

'I c-c-c-can't, s-s-sir,' moaned Nathan.

'Do you want us to leave you on the beach?' barked the teacher.

'N-n-n-no, sir,' wailed Nathan.

'Then I suggest you get up and try and walk.'

So, Nathan, with the help of several pupils, struggled to his feet and attempted to stand, but he soon dropped back down on to the seaweed with a squelch. 'I can't! I can't! It hurts too much!' he howled pathetically.

'Well, here's a pretty kettle of fish,' announced Mr Risley-Newsome irritably. 'After all I have said about keeping off the rocks. You are a silly and disobedient boy, Nathan Thomas.'

'Mr Risley-Newsome,' said Miss Pruitt quietly, 'I am sure that Nathan did not deliberately sprain his ankle. These things do happen. Now, I have asked if I might deal with this. It does not help us all, getting into a state. It is a sprained ankle, nothing more.' Miss Pruitt looked at the wet, shivering children, then up at the ragged grey clouds and out to the cold grey ocean. She felt the chilly, salty wind in her face. The weather looked distinctly ominous. 'I think we should continue. It is getting cold and we still have a mile or so to go. Dominic, will you and Michael help Nathan? Let him put his weight on you.'

'I can't walk on my foot, miss,' wailed Nathan. 'I just can't.'

'Now, look, Nathan,' said Miss Pruitt gently, putting an arm round his shoulder and giving him a warm, motherly smile, 'we really do need to get you off the beach, out of the cold and wet and back to the youth hostel. You understand that, don't you?' The boy nodded. 'It's not that far and if we go slowly and carefully and you lean on Dominic and Michael, we will soon be back home.'

'I'll try, miss,' sniffed the boy, 'but it really does hurt.'

'I'm sure it does, Nathan,' Miss Pruitt told him, squeezing his arm reassuringly. 'It's a nasty sprain. You be a brave boy. Now, come along, let's get moving, shall we?'

With an excruciating expression on his face, Nathan struggled to his feet and wrapped his arms round his two supporters. 'Ooooooh! Ooooooh! Aaaaaaah! Aaaaaaah!' he moaned. 'It's like my foot's coming off.'

'Good,' said Velma under her breath.

'Serves him right,' added Gerald.

'It couldn't have happened to a nicer person,' said Sean.

'Ooooooh! Ooooooh! Aaaaaaah! Aaaaaaah!' Nathan moaned. 'My foot really, really hurts.'

As Dominic helped Nathan hop and limp across the

beach, he could not help feeling rather pleased. After all, Nathan had done nothing but tease and torment him since the trip had begun. He had never missed an opportunity to make a cruel comment or laugh at Dominic. Nathan had now changed his tune and, to Dominic's ears, it was quite a pleasant one.

'Chin up, Nathan!' said Dominic cheerfully. 'Only a couple of miles to go.'

Fourteen

Stranded!

The journey down the beach was slow, very slow indeed. Mr Risley-Newsome strode ahead angrily, then strode back flustered and fidgety and red in the face. 'Can't we go any faster?' he demanded.

'No, we can't,' retorted Miss Pruitt. 'As you can see, the boy's in a lot of pain. He's bruised his knee quite badly and his ankle has swollen up like a balloon. We will just have to carry on slowly but surely until we reach the footpath.'

It sounded to Dominic as if the last sentence was as much to reassure herself that this ordeal would soon be over.

The teacher turned her attention to the injured boy. 'Just think of a nice mug of hot chocolate back at the youth hostel, Nathan, and one of Miss Brewster's scones. Now, come along, let's put a brave face on it, shall we? We'll soon be home.'

And so the children trudged onwards.

The change in the weather was not entirely un-expected. The cold breeze soon turned into an icy and blustery wind that whipped up the waves and blew the sand into ripples. Then it began to rain in earnest. The ragged clouds opened and a grey curtain of water descended, swirling around the children and teachers and soaking them through.

'We really do have to get a move on,' shouted Mr Risley-Newsome, wiping the water from his face before consulting his watch.

'We are going as fast as we can,' said Miss Pruitt sharply.

It was clear to Dominic that she had had just about enough of him barking out orders.

'Perhaps I ought to go on ahead and get help,' suggested Mr Risley-Newsome in a much quieter and more friendly voice. 'I'm sure I could make it back to the youth hostel. I could phone for the emergency services from there.'

'And leave us on the beach?' asked Miss Pruitt.

'I think it's the best course of action,' he told her.

'Well, I don't,' she replied firmly. 'We are not in any imminent danger and by keeping moving we will stay warm. It's best if we all keep together. Perhaps you could take over from the boys.'

'Excuse me?' said Mr Risley-Newsome.

'Take over from the boys,' repeated Miss Pruitt. 'They look just about done in. Maybe you could give Nathan a piggyback. We would make much better time.'

'A piggyback!' cried her colleague.

'We really have to get off the beach, out of this weather. I think we can agree on that, and we would make much faster progress, don't you think, if you carried Nathan on your back?'

Reluctantly Mr Risley-Newsome agreed. Dominic and Michael had quite a job stopping themselves from laughing. Puffing and panting like an exhausted carthorse, Mr Risley-Newsome hauled the heavy, moaning burden on to his back and began crawling down the beach like some giant hermit crab.

Miss Pruitt was too preoccupied to see the funny side. Dominic, when he glanced at his teacher, could tell by her expression how worried she was and the smile soon disappeared from his face.

'Miss, are we going to be all right?' he asked her.

'Of course we are,' she told him, smiling. She didn't sound all that convincing. 'Could you and Velma do something for me?'

'Yes, miss.'

'Run ahead and see how far it is to the path, will you? It can't be far now. Don't go clambering up the cliff. Just run on and see how far we have to go and then run back and tell me. And be careful. We don't want another accident.'

Dominic and Velma ran off, chattering excitedly, kicking sand in every direction like mad donkeys, their faces wet with rain.

'Where are you two going?' shouted Mr Risley-Newsome, as they overtook him.

'Miss Pruitt's asked us to see how much further to the path,' Dominic yelled back without stopping.

The teacher was too tired to argue. His load, soaking wet and clinging on to him like a limpet, was getting heavier and heavier, and Nathan's non-stop moaning in his ear was becoming unbearable.

'I don't know how we'll get Nathan up the cliff,' said Dominic. 'He's really heavy.'

'I can't wait to get into a hot bath with lots of soapsuds,' said Velma, 'and then sit in front of a big roaring fire with that steaming cup of hot chocolate and one of Miss Brewster's home-made scones.'

'And me,' said Dominic.

'It doesn't look as if you'll get a chance to go back to your secret tunnel,' she said, beginning to pant.

'I know,' said Dominic, puffing and blowing by her side. 'I'll be so tired when I get back, I'll fall asleep as soon as my head hits the pillow.'

They were so engrossed in conversation that they didn't realize until the very last moment what was ahead of them.

Velma came to a sudden halt. There was no more sand. 'Where's the beach?' she gasped.

'It's gone,' said Dominic.

In front of them grey floods of water rushed to the shore, covering the sand and crashing against the cliff bottom in a mass of spray and gurgling white foam. Out at sea great green waves curled and arched, moving relentlessly towards them.

'We can't go any further,' said Velma, gripping Dominic's arm so tightly it hurt.

'Oh heck!' he exclaimed. 'We're cut off.'

'We've got a problem, miss,' spluttered Dominic when they had arrived back at the wet and weary crocodile of children and teachers.

'What sort of problem?' demanded Miss Pruitt.

Mr Risley-Newsome, seeing something was amiss, deposited Nathan on a large wet stone with a thud and hurried towards them. 'What is it? What is it?' he barked.

'We're cut off, sir,' said Velma simply.

'What do you mean cut off?' exclaimed the teacher, wiping the water from his face with the flat of his hand.

'Cut off by the sea,' said Dominic. 'We can't go any further. We could see the path leading up the cliffside, but there's no way we can get to it. The tide's come right in.'

'Oh, my goodness,' sighed Miss Pruitt.

'Cut off by the sea?' repeated Mr Risley-Newsome. 'We can't be.'

'We are, sir,' said Dominic. 'The tide's coming in

really fast. It's covered all the sand, so we can't go any further.'

'It's not high tide until later in the afternoon,' mouthed Mr Risley-Newsome. 'It just cannot have come in.'

'Well, it has,' said Dominic, 'and we're cut off.' He stared at Mr Risley-Newsome, waiting for his pronouncement.

'We will have to go back,' the teacher said finally.

'Go back?' whispered Miss Pruitt, moving closer to him so that Dominic and Velma couldn't overhear. 'Of course we can't go back.'

The two children pretended to be fascinated by a seagull being blown across the sky by the icy wind like a scrap of white paper. They were, in fact, listening intently to the teachers' hushed but heated conversation.

'Now, by my reckoning,' Miss Pruitt told Mr Risley-Newsome, 'if we are nearly at the path, we must be directly below the church.'

'No, no, according to my calculations –' began Mr Risley-Newsome.

'Yes we are,' said Miss Pruitt bluntly. 'We must be in the little cove the vicar mentioned. You may not have recalled what the vicar said, but I did. She told us that the cove has two sharp headlands jutting out on either side. Look.' She pointed ahead and then behind her. 'There they are. The vicar said the cliffs curve out like the horns of a bull, just like the ones here and she also said the beach is cut off when the tide is in.

155

And that is exactly what has happened. We're cut off.'

'Oh, dear,' sighed Mr Risley-Newsome.

'Oh, dear, indeed,' repeated Miss Pruitt. 'What a fine mess you have got us into.'

'I never knew your teacher could be like that,' whispered Velma to Dominic. 'She's really angry with him, isn't she?'

'I've never seen her like that either,' Dominic replied. 'Even when I spilt paint all over her, she didn't blow her top.'

'Spilt paint on her?' repeated Velma. 'How did you spill paint on her?'

'It's a long story,' Dominic told her. 'I'll tell you all about it when we get back to the youth hostel.'

'*If* we get back,' said Velma, with a worried look on her face.

The teachers were still arguing.

'How was I to know that we would be delayed by a silly boy hurting his ankle,' Mr Risley-Newsome told Miss Pruitt defensively, pulling a face like a sulking child.

'Mr Risley-Newsome,' said Miss Pruitt, controlling her fury, 'you have told me, endlessly in fact, how well-qualified, knowledgeable and experienced you are, how you have planned everything down to the last detail and how safety conscious you are. You may recall I mentioned the fact that this was a particularly dangerous stretch of beach and there were fast-rising tides, but you assured me –'

'Miss Pruitt,' Mr Risley-Newsome began, holding

up his hand as if stopping traffic, 'this is neither the time nor the place –'

'Don't Miss Pruitt me! Let me finish. Against my better judgement, I agreed to an excursion along what I told you was a notorious stretch of coast, and look where you have got us all – stranded on a deserted beach with the tide coming in. So, Mr Risley-Newsome, what do you suggest we do now?'

'I . . . I . . . I . . . shall have to think,' he replied.

'Well, think quickly, because by the looks of it we haven't much time.'

'I'll go ahead,' he told her, 'and reconnoitre and see if there is a way up the cliffs.' Without waiting for a reply he scurried off.

The rain had stopped and a watery sun appeared from behind an ominously black cloud.

'Children,' said Miss Pruitt, turning to face the group, 'just stop a moment and gather round.' Surrounded by the cluster of wet and shivering children, she smiled bravely. 'We have come across a small problem.' Dominic could tell she was trying to keep up the appearance of calm confidence. 'The path we were to take up to the youth hostel is rather too far for us –'

'No, miss,' interrupted Dominic, 'we're cut –'

'Dominic!' she exclaimed, giving him a knowing look.

He realized by her expression that she did not want any of the pupils to know the truth. Perhaps she thought it would panic them.

'As I said, the path is too far, so Mr Risley-Newsome is exploring other means of getting us off the beach and back home. There's nothing to worry about. So, let's keep moving, shall we?'

She selected two more pupils to help Nathan, and the children continued their laborious trek across the wet and windy beach, following in the deep footprints of Mr Risley-Newsome.

'What were you going to say?' Gerald asked Dominic, running up to walk beside him.

'When?'

'Just now.'

'Nothing.'

'You were. You were going to say that we were cut off by the sea, weren't you?'

'Keep your voice down,' said Dominic. 'Miss Pruitt doesn't want people to know.'

'We're cut off, aren't we?' said Gerald. 'We can't go any further.'

'Yes,' replied Dominic. 'We're cut off.'

'What are we going to do?'

'I don't know,' said Dominic, 'but there is no way we can get to the footpath. There's the whole of the North Sea between us and the way up the cliff.'

'Couldn't we swim for it?' suggested Gerald weakly.

'You should see the sea,' said Dominic. 'And what about Nathan?'

Gerald thought for a moment before replying. 'We could leave him,' he said simply.

Dominic stared at the dark looming cliffs towering

upwards, then at the mounds of brown slimy mud at their base, then at the oily grey ocean crashing on the beach and getting ever closer. The tide was coming in at an alarming rate, rattling the pebbles, sweeping over the sand. Small crabs were appearing out of cracks in the rocks, tiny fish darted in the pools like slivers of glass, starfish emerged from beneath pebbles, all aware that the tide was coming in, and coming in fast.

So absorbed were they in their conversation that neither of the two boys had noticed Darren creeping up behind them and eavesdropping. On hearing the dreadful news he high-tailed it back to Nathan, who was limping slowly down the beach, supported by two boys.

There was suddenly a dreadful strangulated wailing from the invalid, who collapsed on to the sand as if he had been shot. Cradling his sprained ankle, Nathan threw back his head and made again the sound of a frightened animal caught in a snare. His shouts echoed off the cliffs.

'We're going to drown!' he cried. 'We're going to drown!'

The pupils all started to chatter excitedly among themselves.

'We're cut off!' screamed Nathan. 'We can't get off the beach. We're all going to drown!'

'Stop that at once, Nathan Thomas!' Miss Pruitt shouted down the beach. 'There is no question of anyone drowning, so get that silly idea out of your head immediately! And if you open your mouth and make that dreadful noise again, I will give you something to scream about. Now, listen to me everyone. Gather round again, please. We do have a slight problem but really nothing to get in a state about. I want you all to move right back up the beach and shelter in that large cave under the cliffs. Keep well away from the mud and don't go right into the cave, just remain in the entrance out of the wind and rain. Come on, everyone, quickly and sensibly. Darren, you and Sean help Nathan.'

By this time, Mr Risley-Newsome had returned and was standing like a totem pole staring vacantly at the sea. His long pale face was the picture of fear. He looked frozen to the spot.

Having made sure the children were out of the cold and rain, Miss Pruitt took Mr Risley-Newsome's arm and led him a little way down the beach, out of earshot. 'Mr Risley-Newsome,' she said.

'Yes, Miss Pruitt,' he said pathetically.

'I take it there is no way we can get off the beach?'

'We are indeed cut off,' he replied. 'There is just no way ahead of us and the cliffs are too steep and covered in thick mud. I can see the footpath, but there is no way we can get to it. I just don't know what to do.'

Fifteen

The Truth About
Mr Risley-Newsome

Miss Pruitt stared at the figure before her. Gone was all the blustering and boasting, the shouting and swaggering. Mr Risley-Newsome looked quite pathetic – wet, bedraggled, white-faced – she almost felt sorry for him.

If she noticed Dominic standing a little way off, watching her with eyes like saucers and listening to every word, she didn't say anything. She was too concerned with trying to find a way to get out of the predicament that they were all in.

'Right,' she said to Mr Risley-Newsome, taking a deep breath. 'I will tell you what to do. You will go and get help, while I stay here to look after the children.'

Dominic thought she sounded like Mr Merriman speaking to a disobedient pupil. The tables had certainly turned.

'Get help?' protested Mr Risley-Newsome, with a surprised expression on his face.

He looks like a small boy who has just had his lollipop snatched from his hand, Dominic thought.

'That *is* what you wanted to do in the first place, wasn't it?'

'Yes, but that was when I thought there was a way off the beach.'

'I am aware of that,' she told him tartly. 'I suggest you climb up the cliff and summon assistance.'

'Excuse me?'

'Climb up the cliff.'

'That's not possible,' he replied, pulling a horrified face.

'Mr Risley-Newsome,' said Miss Pruitt, speaking slowly and carefully, 'the only way out of this mess – a mess which you have got us into – is for you to climb up the cliff and get help, and the sooner the better.'

Dominic had never seen his teacher quite so forceful. *She is a power to be reckoned with when she gets started*, he thought.

'But the cliffs are slippery and very steep and covered in thick mud,' he said feebly. 'I just wouldn't know how.'

It's about time somebody told him, thought Dominic.

He'd been a pain in the neck from the start of the trip, had 'Old Grisly-Gruesome', telling everybody what to do, shouting at people and all the time with that sour, unpleasant face of his. Dominic had never seen him smile once, except in a sneering, sarcastic way. Dominic grinned to himself. After his gran had tackled the old woman with the chihuahua on Blackpool pier and they were walking up the promenade, she had said that the old woman's face was 'like a smacked bottom'. Mr Risley-Newsome's face was just like that now.

'You have been at great pains since we came to Thundercliff Bay to tell me how inappropriately dressed I am,' Miss Pruitt continued, 'and, of course, I do not have your extensive experience in climbing. You being fully-qualified in outdoor pursuits, orienteering, mountain rescue and survival techniques, I should think you would not find any difficulty in climbing up a cliff. You are clearly the only person capable of attempting it. Certainly I can't, and you are not suggesting a pupil should try, are you?'

'But I haven't a rope or crampons or the correct climbing boots,' he protested, 'and I am rather nervous of heights.'

'Mr Risley-Newsome,' said Miss Pruitt sternly, 'I am telling you to get up those cliffs and summon help. Now!'

'Actually, I've never done any mountain climbing,' he admitted.

'Well, now is your chance to start. Get moving.'

'I really don't think I can,' he said stubbornly.

'Do you want us all to drown?' asked Miss Pruitt. She looked him fiercely in the eyes. 'Well, do you?'

'You don't imagine –' he started.

'It is that serious, Mr Risley-Newsome,' she told him. 'Now, get moving!'

'Very well,' he said.

Dominic watched Mr Risley-Newsome as he picked his way carefully round the rock pools until he stood at the very bottom of the cliff. Then he took a deep breath and began to climb.

All day Dominic had been dreaming about the smugglers and secret passages, galleons and treasure chests. Now, suddenly, he had a far more important thing on his mind. Miss Pruitt's words impressed on him just how serious the situation was and he began to tremble, not knowing whether it was through cold or fear. They were in real trouble, he could see that clearly now. It had never occurred to him that they might actually drown. Now there was a real possibility. Their only means of escape was blocked by deep and dangerous water, the sea was getting closer and closer and the sand disappearing with every rush of the tide. His heart pounded in his chest. Dominic could see the headlines in the papers: 'SCHOOL PARTY WASHED OUT TO SEA' and 'SEA-SIDE TRAGEDY: CHILDREN DROWN'.

'Come along, Dominic,' said Miss Pruitt, walking towards him and putting an arm round his shoulder. 'Up to the cave with the others.'

'I'm frightened, miss,' he said in a small voice.

'We'll be all right,' she replied in a tone that Dominic didn't think was all that convincing.

He joined the children crowding nervously at the mouth of the cave.

'"Old Grisly-Gruesome" has gone for help,' he told his friends. There was a tremble in his voice and he was still shivering. 'It shouldn't be long before he raises the alarm.'

'It better not be,' said Sean, looking out at the angry grey ocean. 'The tide's coming in pretty fast.'

'I reckon it comes right up here,' said Gerald, looking at his feet.

'Do you think it will come into the cave?' asked Velma, nervously.

'I don't know,' said Michael quietly, 'but I don't like the look of it.'

'What do you think, Dom?' asked Sean.

Dominic peered into the cave. His eyes traced the contours in the rock, the shapes and the colours. Then he walked slowly through the entrance and into the shadowy darkness.

'We're not supposed to go inside,' Velma called after him. 'Miss Pruitt said to stay on the beach.'

Dominic wasn't listening. It was as if he was in some sort of trance. He ran his fingers along the slimy walls, kicked the sand underfoot, picked up a piece of dried seaweed and stared this way and that as if he was looking for something or someone. His eyes moved up to the dripping roof. He gazed for what seemed, to his puzzled friends who were watching, to be a long, long time. Then he began nodding, whispering something to himself and finally he gave a great gasp. Running out of the cave, Dominic pushed his way roughly through the pupils and arrived at Miss Pruitt's side. She was watching anxiously the sluggish progress of Mr Risley-Newsome up the muddy cliff face.

'Come on! Come on!' she was saying to herself. 'Do get a move on, Mr Risley-Newsome.'

'Miss! Miss!' Dominic cried excitedly.

'Not now, Dominic, please,' replied Miss Pruitt, her thoughts and eyes focused on the climbing figure.

'But, miss, it's important.'

Miss Pruitt was not listening. 'Mr Risley-Newsome!' she shouted. 'Can you speed up, please. The tide is coming in very fast.'

'Miss!' persisted Dominic. 'Will you listen, please?'

'Dominic, not now! I have enough on my mind at the moment.' She stared again at Mr Risley-Newsome, who was taking slow but steady steps up the cliff face, squelching noisily and heavily in the mud. 'Mr Risley-Newsome!' she shouted again. 'You must hurry.'

'I'm going as fast as I can!' came a peevish voice from the cliff.

Dominic was feeling indignant. For so much of his time in school he seemed to be in trouble – always in Mr Merriman's room for one thing or another, for breaking things, causing accidents, getting into all sorts of scrapes. Now, for once in his life, he knew he could be the one who could really help.

'Will you listen!' he shouted at Miss Pruitt angrily, prodding her arm.

'Dominic!' the teacher replied. 'Don't you dare speak to me like that!'

'But I know a way out, miss!' he cried. 'I know a way off the beach.'

'If only you did,' she replied.

'I do. I really do.' He pulled at the teacher's sleeve. 'Come with me, miss.' He tried to lead her to the cave entrance. 'It's in here, in the cave.'

'No, it's much better that we stay out of the cave. It might fill with water at high tide. We don't want to be trapped in there. We'll wait until Mr Risley-Newsome gets help.'

Almost as if on cue, Mr Risley-Newsome's voice could be heard. 'Help! Help!' he cried. 'I'm stuck. I'm stuck in the mud. I can't move.'

Miss Pruitt rushed down the beach and looked up to see Mr Risley-Newsome clinging to the cliff face like a barnacle, his legs half submerged in the mud.

'Help! Help!' he cried. 'I'm stuck!'

'Oh, for goodness' sake,' she said under her breath. 'Stay there and don't move!' Miss Pruitt shouted back. 'If you start moving you'll sink deeper.'

'Miss!' cried Dominic. He pronounced the next sentence slowly and emphatically. 'I know a way out.'

The teacher looked down at the boy staring up at her and sighed. 'This is not a time for one of your stories, Dominic,' she said softly.

'I know a way out!' he repeated slowly. 'I *really, really* do.'

Miss Pruitt listened to his story. Dominic, in a frantically garbled account, told her about Daisy getting lost and how he had searched for her and discovered the slab of rock and the flight of stone steps leading down to the beach. He told her about the eerie chamber, the overhanging ledge and the cave below and how he had left the rope tied to a tree trunk at the entrance to the tunnel.

'Is this true, Dominic?' she said. 'It sounds to me like one of your weird and wonderful stories.'

'It is true, miss,' he said.

'Dominic,' she sighed, 'even if your story were true, one cave looks just like another.'

'No, no, miss, I'm positive. It *must* be the cave. We're just below the church, right? We could see the footpath ahead of us and that's very nearly below the copse of trees in front of the church, isn't it? Well, this is the only cave on this stretch of beach, so I must be right. Anyway, I recognize it. I just know it is the same cave. If I can climb up on to the ledge, I can go on ahead and find the rope and we'll all be able to get off the beach through the tunnel. Miss, you've got to let me try.'

'Help! Help!' came the plaintive cry of Mr Risley-Newsome, still struggling in the mud.

'Very well, then, Dominic,' the teacher replied, 'and I pray to God that you are right. Come along, let's see this ledge of yours.'

The children watched as Dominic, followed by Miss Pruitt, headed for the cave.

'Miss, what's happening?' moaned Nathan as they passed him.

'Yeah, what's happening, miss?' asked Darren.

'We're trying to find a way out,' Miss Pruitt told them.

'We never will,' Nathan groaned. 'We're all going to drown.'

Miss Pruitt stopped suddenly in her tracks. 'If you start that again, Nathan Thomas,' she exclaimed, 'I'll give you something to moan and groan about. Listen, children,' she said to the shivering group, huddling round the mouth of the cave, staring at her with wide, frightened eyes, 'we think we might have found a way out. Just be a little more patient and, hopefully, we will be soon off the beach and on our way back to the youth hostel.'

Miss Pruitt and Dominic entered the cave and peered around them.

'I can't see how you can be so certain in this light, Dominic –' the teacher began.

'There it is, miss,' said Dominic, pointing up. 'It's up there, look! You can just see the edge of it. Can you see it?'

'I can't see any ledge,' she said, straining her eyes, 'only a bare wall of rock.'

'It's really hard to see from down here,' said Dominic, 'but it's there all right. I know it is.' He shone his torch upwards. 'Can you see it now, miss?'

Miss Pruitt screwed up her eyes as if she were wearing particularly small shoes which pinched her toes. 'No, Dominic, I can't see any ledge. I think you've imagined it.'

'No, no, I haven't, miss,' he cried. 'You can't see it because you don't know where to look. When the customs men were looking for contraband, they couldn't see the ledge either. It's really well hidden. That's how the smugglers managed to get away with all the –'

'Stop it, Dominic!' cried Miss Pruitt. 'This is not the time for one of your far-fetched tales. Your mind is full of smugglers and pirates and I don't know what. There is no ledge, there never was one and I am very angry with you for wasting my time and building up false hopes.' With that she strode out of the cave.

'But, miss,' Dominic called after her, 'there is a ledge.'

Sixteen

Dominic Goes Forth

Dominic ran after Miss Pruitt and gripped her arm. 'Miss,' he pleaded, 'give me a chance.'

'What?' asked the teacher.

'Just give me a chance. I have to show you.'

'Dominic –'

'Please.'

Miss Pruitt thought for a moment and sighed. 'Very well, but it's a waste of time. There's no ledge.'

Miss Pruitt watched Dominic begin to climb the steep cave side, placing each foot, one after the other, into small cracks and indentations in the rock.

'Be careful,' warned the teacher. 'We don't want another accident.'

'What's he doing, miss?' asked Nathan.

'Do be careful, Dominic,' said Miss Pruitt again.

'Miss, what's he doing?' Nathan persisted.

'He's riding a bicycle,' said Sean sarcastically. 'What does it look like he's doing? He's climbing up the side of the cave.'

'Why is he climbing up the wall?' asked Nathan.

'He's finding us a way out, I hope,' said Miss Pruitt, not taking her eyes off the climbing boy.

'What about Mr Risley-Newsome?' asked Velma.

'He can wait for the moment,' replied Miss Pruitt bluntly. 'My main priority is getting you children off the beach.'

Dominic, by this time, had reached the ledge and, pulling himself on to it, disappeared from sight.

'Where's he gone?' asked Nathan.

A moment later Dominic looked down on the teacher and children, a great smile of triumph appearing on his face.

'Good gracious!' exclaimed Miss Pruitt. 'There was a ledge after all.'

Dominic stood with that sort of pioneering triumph which Christopher Columbus, Captain Cook and Scott of the Antarctic must have felt on arriving at their destinations after their difficult journeys. He had found the way out all right and stood there feeling on top of the world.

'This is it!' he cried. 'I knew it was here. I just knew it.' He disappeared and a moment later was back, shouting, 'There are the steps! I can see them!'

Miss Pruitt looked heavenwards. 'Thank you,' she mouthed.

'Shall I climb up to the top, miss, and get help?' asked Dominic.

Miss Pruitt glanced back at the sea, now well up the beach. 'Dominic, does the sea reach up there to the ledge when it comes in? Look on the floor. Is there any dried seaweed or shells or anything like that to show that the tide reaches that high?'

'No, miss, it doesn't. It's just a layer of dry sand and bare rock.'

'Well,' said Miss Pruitt, looking a whole lot happier, 'I think, if there is room for us all, Dominic, the first thing is to get everyone up to where you are and you can then lead us up the steps.'

'There's plenty of room here,' Dominic told her. 'It sort of opens out into a really big space.'

'Splendid!' exclaimed Miss Pruitt.

'Miss, I can't get up there,' moaned Nathan. 'What about my foot?'

'If I have to carry you on my back, Nathan Thomas,' replied Miss Pruitt, 'you will get up there. Now, children, I know you are cold and wet but we will soon be warm and dry and out of all danger. Take off your scarves and anything we can tie together to make a sort of rope which will help us to climb that rock face and on to the ledge where Dominic is. It's not that high.'

'Well, I'm not going up,' mumbled Nathan.

The pupils pulled off their scarves, their excited chatter filling the cave.

Dominic sat on the ledge, letting his legs dangle over. He was feeling pretty pleased with himself.

'What's happening?' came a distant voice from the cliff face.

Miss Pruitt hurried out of the cave and up to the base of the cliff. A figure caked in thick mud was clinging to the branch of a dead tree. 'Mr Risley-Newsome!' she yelled. 'We have found a way off the beach through the cave and I am taking the children back.'

'What?' he shouted.

'I said we have found a way off the beach through the cave and I am taking the children back.'

'What about me?' came a pathetic voice.

'Do you think you could make it down on to the beach?' asked Miss Pruitt.

'No, I can't. I'm stuck in the mud. When I move, I sink deeper.'

'Don't move, then!' she shouted up. 'You stay where you are. I'll get help when we're at the youth hostel.'

'Please hurry, Miss Pruitt. I don't know how much longer I can hold on.'

Back in the cave, Miss Pruitt lined up the children below the ledge. 'Now, I want you to listen carefully,' she said. 'We are having to leave Mr Risley-Newsome here. He's stuck in the mud, but he will be all right.'

174

'If he doesn't move,' Gerald whispered gloomily to no one in particular. 'If he does move, he'll sink. It can suck you under, can mud. He could disappear without a trace.'

'Gerald,' said Miss Pruitt, 'don't be so gruesome.'

Dominic and his friends could not contain a chuckle at the mention of the word 'gruesome'.

'That will do,' said Miss Pruitt. 'There is nothing funny about Mr Risley-Newsome getting stuck in the mud. Now, we are going to tie all the scarves together to make a rope, climb very carefully on to the ledge where Dominic is and go up through a passage to the top.'

'What passage?' asked Nathan.

'Dominic has found a passage,' explained Miss Pruitt.

'How did he know there's a passage?' asked Nathan.

'Never mind how,' said the teacher. 'We haven't all day. Now, come along, everybody, let's get these scarves tied.'

'This is really exciting, miss, isn't it?' Dominic yelled down.

'Only you could say something like that, Dominic,' she said, shaking her head and allowing herself a small smile. 'We are trapped in a cave, with the tide coming in. We are all wet, cold and tired out and you call it exciting.'

Miss Pruitt, turning to the quiet and shivering pupils, told Velma to tie the rope of scarves round her waist and climb up to Dominic. 'Don't rely on it to pull you up,' she told her. 'It's there as a precaution, in case you lose your footing.' Velma slowly climbed up the cave side and clambered up on to the ledge.

'Easy-peasy!' she shouted down.

'Throw one end of the scarf back down,' Miss Pruitt told Velma, 'and you and Dominic hold on to your end very tightly. Michael, you are next. Tie the scarves round your waist and take your time climbing. Off you go.'

One by one the pupils ascended the rock face until there was only Miss Pruitt, Gerald and Nathan left below.

'Come along, Nathan, let's get you up there with the others.'

'I can't, miss. I can't go up there. I know I can't.'

'Come on, Nathan,' said Dominic, 'you can do it.'

'No, no,' he moaned petulantly, 'I can't. I'm frightened, miss. I might fall and break my neck.'

'We are all frightened, Nathan,' said Miss Pruitt, 'but it will soon be over. On your feet. Give me a hand will you please, Gerald.'

'I can't,' said Nathan, beginning to cry.

'Come on, Nathan,' said Gerald. 'Everyone's done it.'

'Well, I can't!' he sobbed.

'Get up!' shouted Velma suddenly, her voice echoing around the cave. 'It's because of your spraining an ankle that we're in this mess. Get off your backside and get moving!'

'Velma!' said Miss Pruitt sharply. 'We can do without that, thank you very much. There's only one teacher here. Come along, Nathan,' she said gently. 'On your feet.'

Gerald and the teacher helped up the whimpering boy and tied the rope of scarves round his waist. He was heaved and hoisted, pushed and pulled until he was with all the other children on the ledge, where he sat quivering and snivelling. Moments later Miss Pruitt and Gerald, accompanied by rousing cheers and whistles which echoed loudly, were there too.

'Just in time, miss,' said Dominic, pointing down.

The sea had now reached the cave entrance and was nibbling at the sand like some great grey creature. Very soon it would swirl into the entrance, crash against the walls, froth and foam and fill the cave's interior.

'Right, children,' said Miss Pruitt, banishing thoughts of what might have happened from her mind, 'let's get out of here.'

Dominic, shining his torch ahead of him, led a line of excited chattering children, like the Pied Piper, all the way up the flight of steps. Miss Pruitt brought up the rear, supporting a groaning and white-faced Nathan.

'It's amazing what a bit of determination can do, isn't it, Nathan?' said the teacher cheerily.

'Yes, miss,' replied Nathan quietly. 'I was really scared.'

'We all were,' she reassured him.

With a little effort and some help, Dominic managed to slide the slab of stone aside sufficiently for him to scramble out. He pushed with all his might until the whole square entrance was exposed, flooding the tunnel with daylight. The rain had now stopped and a cold wind rustled the bushes. He emerged from the darkness, took a deep breath and his face suffused with a great smile of relief. 'We've done it!' he cried. 'We're home!'

Soon they were all out of the tunnel, cheering wildly.

'Let's just calm down, shall we?' said Miss Pruitt. 'We have had a real experience today, an ordeal that we are not likely to forget for some time. You have all been absolutely wonderful, brave and well behaved and I am very proud of you.' There was more than one listener who gave Nathan a sideways glance at these words. 'Now, let's make our way, sensibly, to the youth hostel. I want you all to get out of your wet things, put on some dry clothes and meet me in the library in fifteen minutes. I will arrange for a hot drink and something to eat. Best behaviour, please. I need to see to Nathan's foot.'

Wet, dishevelled and weary, but still chattering excitedly, the pupils made their way across the grass at the rear of the youth hostel.

On the way Miss Pruitt, with Nathan limping beside her, caught up with Dominic. 'You were brilliant, Dominic,' she said, and she squeezed his shoulder and smiled. Velma nudged Sean and they smiled too. 'I could give you a great big hug, I really could.'

'Please don't, miss!' Dominic exclaimed, looking decidedly uneasy. 'That would be taking things a bit too far.'

Once inside the youth hostel, Miss Pruitt, having deposited Nathan on a chair in the warm kitchen, with Dominic, Velma and Darren to keep him company, went in search of Miss Brewster.

'I thought I'd never get off that beach,' wailed Nathan. His body began to shake uncontrollably and great tears streamed down his grubby cheeks. 'I really thought we'd drown. I . . . I . . . was –' He couldn't finish the sentence but sat there crying and trembling.

What a picture he presented, thought Dominic. The bragging, cruel-tongued tormentor was now a blubbering, pathetic, trembling figure hunched in the chair like an old man. His teasing days were over. He would never wish to be reminded of his behaviour on the beach.

'Well, it's over now, Nathan,' said Dominic gently. He rested his hand on the boy's shoulder, recalling one of his gran's expressions: 'Never kick a man when he's down'.

'Yes, it's over now,' echoed Darren, who had recently taken to repeating Dominic. 'All over now.'

'We're all safe,' said Dominic. 'That's the main thing.'

'All safe,' said Darren.

'Thanks to Dominic,' added Velma. She did not feel quite as charitable towards Nathan.

'Yeah, thanks to Dominic,' repeated Darren.

179

Miss Brewster, followed by Miss Pruitt, bustled into the kitchen.

'I was beginning to get worried,' Miss Brewster was telling the teacher. 'You were overdue. I was about to give the police a call. I know how cold and wet it can get out there at this time of year. Now, where's the invalid?' She examined the ankle. 'Oh, not too bad, just a nasty sprain, I think. Better get you to the hospital just to be on the safe side, though. I'll run him in if you like, Miss Pruitt. Perhaps you'd like to come. I'm sure Mr Risley-Newsome will be able to manage on his own.'

'Mr Risley-Newsome!' gasped Miss Pruitt. 'I forgot all about him. He's still stuck in the mud!'

Epilogue

Later that day Mr Risley-Newsome, bent and mud-caked, looking like the 'Creature from the Black Lagoon', shuffled across the grass at the rear of the youth hostel between his two rescuers. The air-sea rescue team had been called out and he had been winched off the cliff face by helicopter and delivered back to the youth hostel in this sad and sorry state.

The police had been none too pleased with him and he had received a good telling-off in the library, with all the children listening in at the door.

'It beggars belief,' the policeman had told him sternly, 'that supposedly responsible teachers should even consider taking children on such a dangerous stretch of coast, particularly at this time of year and in weather like this. Thundercliff Wyke is notorious. It's extremely rocky, very secluded, there are falling rocks, shifting sands, mountains of sinking mud and fast-rising tides. It's a recipe for disaster. There are signs right along that coast. All the guide books mention how dangerous it can be. Even on a fine day, conditions can rapidly change, and you take children across a deserted beach in November! It only takes a freak wave or the tide to come in quickly for people to get into trouble, to be swept away, fall off crumbling cliffs, be cut off or end up stuck in the mud. Did you not think of checking all this before you set off?'

Dominic could visualize Miss Pruitt sitting there in silence, with an expression which said 'I told you so'.

'And if you *will* climb mountains and walk in deserted areas,' the policeman continued, 'you would be well advised to wear something bright. We would have found you a whole lot sooner if you had been dressed like the other teacher.'

That evening, after dinner, Mr Risley-Newsome stood at the library window, looking across the endless sea, now calm and silver in the moonlight. The two great headlands at the ends of the crescent of sand rose hump-backed like great marine creatures emerging from the still water. Silhouetted against the empty sky, they looked black and foreboding.

'May I come in, sir?' It was Dominic.

'What is it, Dowson?'

'I just want to return this book.'

'Return it, then.'

The teacher stared out again at the ocean. He shuddered. In his mind's eye he saw the most terrifying picture. The cold grey ocean sweeping relentlessly up the beach, its icy arms enfolding the children, tugging them down, down, down to the watery depths.

'Are you all right, sir?' asked Dominic.

'Of course I'm all right,' he snapped. 'Get about your business.'

Of course, he was far from all right. He had been made to look a fool; he felt humiliated. Mr Risley-Newsome knew he would never be quite the same again.

Just before the children got ready for bed, Miss Pruitt stood at the window in the games' room. What a week it had been. What a memorable week. Talk about excitement, thrills, action and humour. She smacked her hand to her mouth to stifle a laugh. Poor Mr Risley-Newsome. She thought of the sight of him, covered from head to toe in mud, completely brown save for the whites of his eyes, arriving at the door of the youth hostel like some ponderous creature which had crawled out of a swamp. Then, later, he had stood there before the policeman like a naughty schoolboy in front of the headteacher. She knew it was not charitable to laugh at another's misfortunes (she had told the children that often enough), but she couldn't restrain herself.

'Ha ha ha,' she chortled.

'Are you all right, miss?' asked Dominic, looking up from his game of chess with Velma.

'Of course, I'm all right,' she replied. 'I'm as right as rain.'

But she was far more than all right, for Miss Pruitt had discovered something about herself – that in a real crisis she could keep her head, organize her pupils and take charge of the situation. She, too, would never be quite the same again.

After lights out, Dominic stood at his bedroom window. As he surveyed the vast expanse of water, he thought of the smugglers of old, crouching over their muffled oars, rowing ashore, riding the waves with the sea spray in their faces, wading ashore carrying their heavy cargo. He heard the scrape of the boat as they heaved it across the pebble-strewn beach. He heard the boots crunching, saw the lanterns glowing in the darkness, smelt the salty tang in his nostrils. And he thought of the secret tunnel, the steep slippery steps, the empty chamber, the flickering torches casting ghostly shadows on the roof.

Dominic had been disappointed to learn that night that he had not been the first to have discovered the tunnel. The police had known of it, so had Miss Brewster and the vicar. It had, in fact, been common knowledge to the residents of Thundercliff Bay for many, many years. But it had been a well-kept secret because, as Miss Brewster had explained to him, they did not want inquisitive children getting lost underground or trapped or breaking their necks on the slippery steps. Many had looked for treasure, she had gone on to tell him, people from the museum and from the university, archaeologists and potholers, all manner of folk, and they had found not so much as a brass farthing. 'There's no treasure down there, Dominic,' she had said. 'It will have disappeared long ago.'

'There is treasure down there, I just know there is,' he said under his breath now. 'And one day I'll return and find it.'

As he spoke the words, he looked down at the small golden disc in the palm of his hand. It glinted in the moonlight. He had found the coin, picked out in the light of his torch, as he had led the way up through the tunnel from the beach. On one side it had the date, 1797, written above a shield, shaped like a spade on a playing card. On the other was the profile of a king with a tangle of curly hair and the words: GEORGIUS III DEI GRATIA. It was a golden guinea. And Dominic knew just the person to give it to.

He looked at the sea shimmering silver in the moonlight. 'Not so much as a brass farthing,' he said smiling. 'Well, I know better.'

www.puffin.co.uk.www.puffin.co.uk.www.puffin.co.uk

bookinfo.competitions.news.games.sneakpreviews

www.puffin.co.uk.www.puffin.co.uk.www.puffin.co.uk

adventure.bestsellers.fun.coollinks.freestuff

www.puffin.co.uk.www.puffin.co.uk.www.puffin.co.uk

explore.yourshout.awards.toptips.authorinfo

www.puffin.co.uk.www.puffin.co.uk.www.puffin.co.uk

greatbooks.greatbooks.greatbooks.greatbooks

www.puffin.co.uk.www.puffin.co.uk.www.puffin.co.uk

reviews.poems.jokes.authorevents.audioclips

www.puffin.co.uk.www.puffin.co.uk.www.puffin.co.uk

interviews.e-mailupdates.bookinfo.competitions.news

www.puffin.co.uk

games.sneakpreviews.adventure.bestsellers.fun

www.puffin.co.uk.www.puffin.co.uk.www.puffin.co.uk

bookinfo.competitions.news.games.sneakpreviews

www.puffin.co.uk.www.puffin.co.uk.www.puffin.co.uk

adventure.bestsellers.fun.coollinks.freestuff

www.puffin.co.uk.www.puffin.co.uk.www.puffin.co.uk

explore.yourshout.awards.toptips.authorinfo

www.puffin.co.uk.www.puffin.co.uk.www.puffin.co.uk

greatbooks.greatbooks.greatbooks.greatbooks

www.puffin.co.uk.www.puffin.co.uk.www.puffin.co.uk

reviews.poems.jokes.authorevents.audioclips

www.puffin.co.uk.www.puffin.co.uk.www.puffin.co.uk